The carpet on the stairs was tattered and worn; holes had opened in the fabric and flaps of the carpet had come loose, so the girls had to be careful not to trip on their way up. They moved slowly, carefully; occasionally a step would creak, making one of them flinch or utter a sharp little gasp.

Bret asked, ''Want to go on up to the workroom?''

They headed up the next flight of stairs to the attic. Erika opened the door. It moved stiffly, and she had to lean on it hard to get it all the way open. Once she'd succeeded, they walked in.

The door began to squeak shut behind Leslie, the last one in the room.

Flashlight beams moved over the once-cluttered worktables, over the old clothes hanging on the rack encased in cobwebs, and—a rusted ax stuck in the middle of the wood floor beside a pile of amputated arms and legs.

The darkness filled with screams.

PETRIFIED

Joseph Locke

BANTAM BOOKS
NEW YORK · TORONTO · LONDON · SYDNEY · AUCKLAND

*This book is dedicated to
my dog
Tucker*

RL 6, age 12 and up

PETRIFIED

A Bantam Book / February 1992

The Starfire logo is a registered trademark of Bantam Books,
a division of Bantam Doubleday Dell Publishing Group, Inc.
Registered in U.S. Patent and Trademark Office and elsewhere.

ISBN 0-553-29657-4

Published simultaneously in the United States and Canada

Bantam Books are published by Bantam Books, a division of Bantam Doubleday
Dell Publishing Group, Inc. Its trademark, consisting of the words "Bantam
Books" and the portrayal of a rooster, is Registered in U.S. Patent and Trade-
mark Office and in other countries. Marca Registrada. Bantam Books, 666 Fifth
Avenue, New York, New York 10103.

PRINTED IN THE UNITED STATES OF AMERICA

RAD 0 9 8 7 6 5 4 3 2 1

Acknowledgments

For their help and support, I'd like to thank my editor, Diana Ajjan; my agent, Lori Perkins; and my wife, Logan.

PROLOGUE

An ice-cold rain fell as the four girls walked and skipped, giggling and chattering beneath two umbrellas, down a quiet street in Dinsmore, the town they would all be leaving soon. It was the first day of their Christmas vacation, and the houses and apartment buildings they passed had twinkling lights around their windows and colorful wreaths on their doors.

None of the girls mentioned their impending departures, all of which would be at various times and for various reasons. Instead, they enjoyed their walk and spoke of the coming school year as if they would be entering their sixth-grade year the way they had entered the five before it: together. They behaved as if they would always be the closest of friends, always live in close proximity to one another, just blocks apart in their hometown.

The girls were going to one of their favorite places together. While the other kids in town gathered at the mall or Skatetown or the Milky Way Arcade, *they* went to the Waxhouse, where old Mr. and Mrs. Wattenberg, the owners, were always happy to take them into the workroom for some herbal tea and a look at the progress of their newest creations. The Wattenbergs hadn't charged them admission in over a year. The girls didn't go every day, but they tried not to let too much time pass between visits. It had been ten days since they'd last dropped in on Mr. and Mrs. Wattenberg.

With Erika walking slightly ahead and the others—Lynda, Bret, and Leslie—gathered just behind her, they stopped across Barton Road from the Waxhouse.

"I've got a sweet tooth," Leslie chirped. "Let's go over to Broussard's first." She nodded toward Broussard's Market, which was across the intersection diagonally.

It was an old market, but Ted Broussard—whose father had turned it over to him just before dying—and his wife managed to keep it up in spite of their herd of children, to which Mrs. Broussard would be adding another soon.

Checking for traffic first, the girls dashed across the intersection and onto the store's gravel lot, darting around the four gas pumps beneath a small canopy rimmed with plastic multicolor flags that fluttered in the breeze. There they got some chewing gum and Red Hots and M&M's and Sweet Tarts. At the counter Mrs. Broussard had to reach over her growing belly to operate the register, at the same time shouting over her shoulder to her children, who were arguing noisily in the back room.

"How much longer?" Erika asked with a smile, nodding toward Mrs. Broussard's belly.

"Oh, about two months," the woman said wearily. "But I know better than to expect them on time."

"You gonna have more after this?" Bret asked.

"Maybe so, but not here."

The girls looked at her with surprise. "You're moving?" Lynda asked.

Mrs. Broussard nodded. "Soon as we sell the store. Who knows how long that will take. That all for you today?"

The girls said their good-byes, took their candy, and left, hurrying across the street to the Waxhouse.

It was an enormous, three-story Victorian home that, years ago, had been located in the busiest part of Dinsmore. The house hadn't been moved; the town had changed. The older shops around the Waxhouse closed up one at a time as newer and better stores began opening up at the northern end of town. Then the

3

mall opened in Eureka, taking away even more business, and what old shops remained there closed up and were eventually torn down to make room for apartment buildings, tract houses, and a couple of convenience stores. Only the Waxhouse and Broussard's Market remained, and now it seemed even the market could be on its way out.

Being a seaside town, Dinsmore was often visited by the tourists who flocked to the northern California coast, and many of them still patronized the Waxhouse. But business was not what it used to be, and it dropped a little more every year as Mr. and Mrs. Wattenberg got older and it became more difficult for them to care for the big old house.

"It doesn't look like there are any customers here," Erika said, noticing the long deserted curbs around the house where customers usually parked their cars. It made her feel sad to see business die down for the Wattenbergs. They were such nice people and had been so good to Erika and her friends.

Lynda said, "Maybe it's a slow day."

"Aw, come on," Bret said in her usual low voice that bordered on a grumble. "It's *always* a slow day. Nobody comes here anymore but us."

As they started up the cobblestone walk that led to the front steps and the vast covered porch, Leslie said, "I bet if they just fixed it up

4

a little, you know? I mean, maybe some new paint? A little yard work? Know what I mean? I bet some flowers along the path would—"

"Stop it, Leslie!" Erika hissed over her shoulder. Then she turned to face them on the porch and said, "Come on, you guys, quit saying those things. The Wattenbergs are doing the best they can. They're old, and they—"

The double doors opened behind her, and Erika spun around to see Emerick Wattenberg smiling at them from the large doorway. Even with the slouched posture imposed on him by old age, he still was a tall, broad man, still appeared to have strength in his shoulders, and still walked with an assured, proud step. He held out his big hands, fingers thin and graceful but for the knobby, arthritic knuckles, and beckoned them inside with a rich laugh.

"Come in, young ladies, come in," he said, stepping aside as they entered.

As Mr. Wattenberg closed the doors, the girls went past the box office and passed through the red velvet curtains that led into the first section of the wax museum.

There were six theme rooms throughout the enormous house, and the girls walked into the first: Great Moments in History. The Wattenbergs were constantly working on new wax figures and replaced the figures in each room with new ones on a regular basis. On display in the history room at that time were scenes featuring Napoleon Bonaparte atop a beautiful horse, Genghis Khan raising a sword in battle, Joan of Arc listening intently to silent voices, Thomas Jefferson and Benjamin Franklin arguing over the Constitution, and, most impressive of all, but made even more so by some very creative and elaborate lighting, the crucifixion of Christ.

The crucifixion scene was new, and the girls had never seen it before. They went to it immediately and whispered comments to one another as they stared up at Christ's bloody, agonized face.

"Do you like it?" Mr. Wattenberg asked.

"It's beautiful," Erika said.

"Yes, we worked long and hard on that one."

They heard footsteps coming down the stairs, and in a moment Ellie Wattenberg appeared, a short, silver-haired woman growing rounder all the time. She wore small silver-rimmed spectacles and tilted her head forward to look over the top of them at the girls.

Mrs. Wattenberg offered to take them upstairs to the workroom for tea, but the girls wanted to see any new wax figures first, so she and her husband led them through the house.

They skipped the American Leaders room.

"We've stopped adding to that one since we put in Martin Luther King, Junior," Mr. Wattenberg said.

His wife nodded. "We're going to change it

to movie stars. Far as we can tell, there are no more leaders.''

The new addition in the Fantasy room was Bilbo Baggins and Gandalf the wizard from Tolkien's *The Hobbit*. Upstairs in Great Scenes from Literature, they'd added Sherlock Holmes and Dr. Watson on the trail of *The Hound of the Baskervilles*. Next door they had added Holmes's creator, Sir Arthur Conan Doyle, to their collection of great authors.

''There are a few new ones in the basement,'' Mr. Wattenberg said with a mischievous gleam in his eye, ''if you'd like to see them.''

Erika declined at once. The basement held the Chamber of Horrors. They had gone down there once before, and that had been more than enough for Erika. It was dark and chilly, and a hidden speaker played eerie music and sound effects to add to the already frightening atmosphere. Cobwebs filled the corners, and old movie monsters lurked in the darkness among gravestones and hooting owls with flickering eyes. As if that hadn't been enough, Bret had crept ahead of them and hidden in a dark corner with the cape she'd removed from Count Dracula's back, and when the other girls passed, she'd jumped out at them with a shriek and sent them all running in the other direction, terrified. Yes, Erika had seen it before, and it had given her the creeps, so she didn't care to see it again, even if there *were* new figures down there.

"Oh, come on," Bret said. "We haven't been down there in a while. Let's go take a look."

"So you can scare the pants off of us again?" Erika asked.

"Yeah," Leslie added. "That was a rotten thing to do last time. What a dink."

"I won't do it again," Bret said sincerely. "Really."

Bret glanced up at Mr. Wattenberg. Erika wasn't sure, but she *thought* she'd seen the old fellow give Bret a conspiratorial wink.

"Uh-uh," Erika said, shaking her head decisively. "I know you, Bret. I know what you'll do."

"She said she wouldn't." Lynda spoke up. "I believe her."

"Then you go," Leslie said.

"No, really." Lynda sounded serious. "I think it would be fun to go down into the Chamber of Horrors again, and I believe Bret when she says she won't do anything to scare us."

Leslie turned her head slowly to Erika. "Well? What do you think?"

Erika's mouth dropped open. "You believe her? Are you *nuts*?"

Leslie shrugged. "I think it'd be fun. Besides, it'll probably be our last chance. And so what if she does do something?" she asked, tossing a glance at Bret. "We'll know it's Bret. We know there's nothing down there that can hurt us."

Erika sighed and rolled her eyes, defeated.

8

"Oh, all right. Let's go look at the new monsters downstairs."

With a hearty laugh Mr. Wattenberg led the girls downstairs while Mrs. Wattenberg went to the workroom to prepare tea.

"Don't you frighten those girls down there," the old woman called over her shoulder to her husband.

"Won't need to," he said. "I suspect they'll frighten themselves."

As they went through the basement door and headed down the stairs, they heard the creepy horror movie music, the sound effects—wind blowing, rain falling, thunder clapping, and wolves howling in the distance—and the occasional sinister laugh of some fiend lurking around a corner in the dark. The tape had been changed since their last visit. This one was worse.

They were still there, waiting in the dark: Frankenstein's monster, the Wolfman, a mummy, and Dracula, illuminated by concealed multicolor lights.

"And this is one of our new ones," Mr. Wattenberg said, waving his arm in a grand gesture toward an executioner, muscular and shirtless, wearing a black hood over his head and holding a deadly ax high above him. The victim was on his knees, hands tied behind his back, head on a large block awaiting its liberation.

The girls commented on the craftsmanship, but couldn't hide a slight shudder.

Mr. Wattenberg led them deeper into the basement to show them the newest addition: the Phantom of the Opera.

"The Lon Chaney phantom," he said, nodding toward the figure with its long, skeletal face and mangled teeth. "The best one of the lot."

Once again the girls remarked on the good work, but could not say anything *too* nice; it was simply too ugly.

The rear of the basement was much darker; there were no lights illuminating the wax figures . . . there was just darkness. It took the girls a few moments to realize that a black curtain had been hung to close off a section of the room.

"We're going to be making some changes back here," Mr. Wattenberg said. "That's why we've got this curtain up. We're planning a torture chamber. Of course, we'll have to put up some paneling to cover the window near the corner and block out the light." He stepped over to the curtain and parted it, and—

A growling figure dived through the opening wearing a black hood and holding an enormous ax over its head.

The girls screamed at the top of their lungs, spun around, and ran back toward the stairs. They were halfway up to the door when they realized Bret was not with them. When they stopped running and their feet stopped clattering on the steps, they heard her laughing behind them.

Erika took a few steps back down and saw the executioner; his hood and ax were gone.

Bret came down the aisle that ran through the center of the gallery of monsters swinging the balsa wood ax and laughing. "I got you good this time!"

"You said you wouldn't!" Lynda cried.

"And you believed her," Erika grumbled.

Mr. Wattenberg joined them, laughing. "Don't take it so hard, girls," he said. "Be glad you can enjoy such a fright. Someday, when you're my age, it could very well kill you."

They went back upstairs and joined Mrs. Wattenberg in the workroom for tea and a snack.

The workroom—a converted attic—was at once magical and eerie. Bodies in various stages of development were everywhere. Arms and legs, heads and torsos were scattered throughout the large room. Graceful, disembodied hands lay on tables. Gruesomely realistic eyeballs were lined up on shelves. Wigs and toupees crouched on faceless Styrofoam heads like strange small animals ready to pounce. Colorful, extravagant clothes from times past hung on a rack that ran along the far wall. Then there were the tools hanging on racks in the work area, exotic instruments, some intriguing, others no less scary than a dentist's drill or a pirate's hook. Directly opposite the door was an elevator the Wattenbergs had installed many years ago so that, after pouring the molds in the furnace room behind the house, Mr. Wattenberg could bring the figures up to the attic without having to haul them up the stairs. In one corner of the room was a small refrigerator and a kettle of hot water on a portable burner.

—Mrs. Wattenberg sliced a pound cake and made cinnamon tea while her husband brought some folding chairs from a closet.

Once they were all seated and each held a steaming cup of tea, they began to talk about the usual things: what the girls had been doing with their summer, how things were going at home, and, of course, Karin.

"We still haven't seen her," Erika said.

Leslie added, "And her mother won't let any of us talk to her on the phone."

"She's always nice enough," Lynda said. "She just says Karin is in no condition to talk with anyone. She *always* says that."

"Is the girl ill?" Mr. Wattenberg asked.

The girls exchanged glances and didn't answer at first. They had their theories.

Karin Potter had been a member of their little group since they'd been together. Over the last couple of years they'd watched Karin, a chubby girl with a round face, become more and more withdrawn and odd—even more than she'd been when they'd first spoken to

12

her. Her mind seemed to wander sometimes, until it was almost as if she weren't there with them. Then, one day six months ago, Karin's mother—who was a bit odd herself, with a sinister scar that started just below her right eye and went all the way down to the line of her jaw—had withdrawn Karin from school to be tutored at home. None of them knew why. They hadn't seen or heard from Karin since then.

Erika opened her mouth to answer Mr. Wattenberg's question, but hesitated.

"We think she's mentally ill," Bret said suddenly.

Erika and the others scowled at her.

"Is that true?" Mrs. Wattenberg asked, leaning forward and frowning with concern.

"Well," Erika said, "it's what we think. We're not *sure*, but . . . well, it kind of looks like that."

Mrs. Wattenberg sat back in her chair as she shook her head and clicked her tongue. "What a shame. What a terrible shame."

They were silent a while, then Erika said, "This is sort of a special occasion for us." She spoke quietly. None of them had been looking forward to telling the Wattenbergs that this was probably their last visit.

The old couple's faces brightened, and Mr. Wattenberg said, "Is that a fact? And what *is* the occasion?"

"Well," Erika said, "it's sort of a . . . *sad* special occasion. See, this is the last time we'll all be here together. I mean, we're not really all together *now* with Karin gone, but this is the, um . . . well . . . we're all going to be leaving."

"Leaving?" Mrs. Wattenberg asked.

"Town?" Mr. Wattenberg asked.

The girls nodded.

Mrs. Wattenberg said, "You're all leaving *together*? Is it some kind of field trip?"

They laughed.

"It just worked out that way," Lynda explained. "We're not leaving at the same time, but we'll be gone by the time school starts."

"And we're all going for different reasons," Bret added. "Like me, I'm going with my mom because she says she doesn't even want to live in the same town as my dad after the divorce is over."

"You mean when it's final," Erika said.

"Whatever. So we'll be going up the coast somewhere, she says. Probably Oregon. Where I hope to grow up fast and get married so I don't have to live with this last name anymore."

Mrs. Wattenberg laughed. "You're still going on about your last name? I don't see what's wrong with it."

"Woinowski? It's a *gross* last name."

"I'm leaving because of my dad," Lynda said, bouncing in her chair. She was normally a bub-

14

bly girl, but when she spoke of her father's recent accomplishment, she could scarcely contain herself, and her enthusiasm doubled. Her father was a sculptor whose work, especially in the last three years, had been getting a great deal of attention. "Daddy's been asked to go teach at some art school in Paris," Lynda went on. "And there's a famous gallery there that wants to show his work."

Leslie said, "My mom's doctor told her she couldn't live here anymore because her lungs have gotten so bad. He says they're never going to get better because of her disease, but she could at least slow the process down by moving to a drier climate. So we're going to Arizona."

Mr. and Mrs. Wattenberg turned to Erika. Their eyes looked so hurt.

"And what about you," Mrs. Wattenberg said quietly. "Where are you going, Erika, dear?"

"Southern California," she replied. "My dad is being transferred to a plant down there." He was an engineer who designed fishing boats at a plant just outside of nearby Eureka. "He's going to be designing sailboats for racing. He's excited because it means more money and it's a better job, but . . ." She looked around at all of them and shrugged, then whispered, "I don't really want to leave."

"Of course you don't," Mr. Wattenberg said. "That's understandable."

Mrs. Wattenberg's sad face was broken by a bright smile. "But think of the fun you'll have going to new places and meeting new people. And you'll all stay in touch with each other and come visit us here in the summers if you can, right? How does that sound?"

The girls all smiled and nodded, then sipped their tea silently.

There was a sound from downstairs. Faint. A door closing. Footsteps. Then a voice . . .

"I think we have a customer," Mr. Wattenberg said, going to the door. He opened it and called, "Be right down."

Before he could start down the stairs, a familiar voice said, "Mr. Wattenberg?"

"Karin, honey?" he asked. "That you?"

The girls put down their tea and hurried to Mr. Wattenberg's side, gathering around the open door and looking down the stairs. When they saw her climbing slowly toward them, they were shocked. It *was* Karin! As she came up, she kept glancing over her shoulders nervously until she'd reached the top and came into the workroom.

Her clothes were horribly wrinkled and didn't match. Her mousy brown hair was a mess, spiking out in some spots and sticking to her head in others. She looked around at them and gave a half-smile, then bowed her head, embarrassed.

Mrs. Wattenberg hugged her. "We've *missed*

16

you, dear! Where have you been? Have you been well?''

With a tiny, timid smile, Karin shook her head ever so slightly.

The girls moved forward and surrounded her. Erika said, ''Well, we're glad you're here now.''

''I . . . I heard you were all . . . leaving,'' she whispered.

They nodded.

''I-I wanted to see you all. One more time.'' There was a tension in her brow that didn't seem to go away and became worse with each word she spoke.

The girls took turns hugging her while Mrs. Wattenberg poured her some tea. They spent most of the afternoon browsing around the workroom, looking at the clothes that hung on the rack, toying with the wax body parts scattered over the worktables, and making each other wince and flinch with the eyeballs.

As the time passed, Karin slowly changed. The girls noticed it, but didn't say anything as she grew more quiet and withdrawn. After a while her eyes began to dart around nervously, and her lips moved as if she were muttering under her breath. Erika and the others exchanged glances as Karin finally withdrew to a shadowy corner of the large room and hunkered down on the wood floor.

''Karin?'' Mrs. Wattenberg called. ''What's wrong, sweetheart? Are you all right?''

No response.

"What's the matter, Karin?" Mr. Wattenberg asked.

When Karin continued to remain silent, the girls moved toward her together, surrounding her in the corner. They spoke softly.

"Is there something we can do for you, Karin?" Erika asked.

"Do you want some more tea?" Lynda asked.

Before anyone else could speak, Karin shot to her feet and screamed, "I want you to stop *lying* to me!"

The girls flinched and stumbled backward, shocked. Karin's eyes were wide, her lips pulled back over her teeth. She looked like a different person entirely, and the sudden drastic change frightened not only the girls, but the Wattenbergs, too.

"Stop pretending you *like* me," Karin went on, "when you really *hate* me! When you really *laugh* at me behind my *back*! You *laugh* at me and *talk* about me behind my *back*. You hate me because I'm too *ugly* and too *fat*, because my clothes aren't pretty and my hair isn't done nice, because I'll *never* fit in with your friends, so I can *never* fit in with *you*, and I'll *never* be *pretty* like *you*! I'll never have *real* friends! You don't *really* want me around—you just want me around so you can *laugh* at me! I'm your pet *charity*! Your own little *joke*!" She collapsed back in the corner, this time sobbing.

18

She hugged her legs to her and buried her head between her knees as her shoulders quaked with sobs.

The girls looked at one another, mouths hanging open. Mr. and Mrs. Wattenberg simply stared, at a loss.

Erika suddenly felt sick to her stomach. Had *she* caused this? Had what she'd said to Karin last year caused the change in her, caused *this*? She hoped not, prayed not. She was the first to move forward. She knelt beside Karin and whispered, "That's not true, you know. None of that's true. You *are* our friend. We *love* you. And we would never talk about you or laugh at you like you said. Never. Maybe other people have done that, but not us." It was a lie, but just a tiny one, a white one. "Please believe me, Karin. We *are* your friends. If we weren't, we wouldn't miss you when you're not around. We do, you know."

Karin stopped crying suddenly and lifted her head. She looked around with a surprised expression, as if she'd just awoke to find herself in a strange place. She looked at each of them, then got to her feet. She scrubbed her face with both hands, then stammered, "I-I-I'm sorry. Really. I mean, I . . . I didn't, um . . . I . . ."

"Oh, that's okay, darling," Mrs. Wattenberg said, stepping forward. She put an arm around Karin. "Don't you think anything of it."

"Yeah," Lynda said, grinning. "You were just upset, is all."

"I really am sorry," Karin whispered to the girls. "I . . . I didn't . . . mean any of that. I-I don't even know why I—"

Mrs. Wattenberg patted her shoulder. "Shh-sh."

There was a long, uncomfortable pause until Erika stepped forward.

"Let's make a pact," she said, taking Karin's hand. "Everybody hold hands. Come on."

Bret rolled her eyes.

"Come *on*, Bret," Erika said. "It doesn't count if you don't. Okay . . . everybody holding hands? Okay. On this day, let's see . . . just before our senior year, so that'll be . . . okay, on this day, six years from now, we will all meet here, at the Waxhouse, no matter *where* we are, no matter *how* far we have to travel. That way," she said with a smile, "no matter how many miles separate us, we'll always know we're going to be together again . . ."

Countless letters and long-distance telephone calls clocked the passing of the years after their separation. They told one another about their activities, the new friends they made, family squabbles, boyfriends, and, of course, how much they hated school.

At the beginning of Leslie's junior year, her mother finally surrendered to her illness and died. Leslie wrote no letters for a while because she was spending so much time with her fam-

20

ily. Finally she began calling her long-distance friends for their support.

Lynda's family returned from Europe and settled in Westchester, a suburb of New York, where Lynda's father took a teaching job at a prominent art school.

Erika and Bret, on the other hand, continued their lives without any great upheaval.

While the four girls were faithful about staying in touch with one another, none of them heard from Karin, neither by phone nor by letter. Concerned, each of the girls wrote to her, but received no response. They called her, but got nothing more than an answering machine with Karin's mother's recorded voice asking them to leave a message. They always left messages, but Karin never called back.

During their conversations and in their letters, the girls wondered about Karin and speculated about what was going on. Had she gotten worse? Had her apparent mental illness grown serious enough to require hospitalization? Or, worse yet, institutionalization?

When they weren't talking on the phone with one another, the girls wondered other things about Karin, things they didn't want to share with the others. Things about which each girl was not very proud—not now, anyway, after the passage of time had given her the opportunity to reconsider.

Because each girl had a little secret, and each secret involved Karin. And the girls hoped that, as more time passed, their secrets would pass with it, so they wouldn't have to feel the small, hot blade of guilt in their chests anymore.

Time passed, but their secrets did not. Their guilt would only grow worse.

ONE

Arrivals

Erika smiled as she drove into Dinsmore because it was raining again, and a cold winter breeze blew beneath the steel gray sky. It was just like the weather six years ago that very day.

She drove through town and looked for the inevitable changes. The Milky Way Arcade was now a video store, and three blocks down and across the street, Skatetown had become a Nautilus club. But although she'd expected to see that a new theater had opened, the Vogue Theater was still in business and showing third-run double features every Friday and Saturday. That meant that anyone who wanted to see a new movie had to drive fifteen miles south to Eureka. Cochran's Hardware was still open, and so were the Frostee Kone, Comicorner, and Burger Barrel. Somehow she'd expected things to look a lot different when she arrived.

"It's only been six years," she muttered to herself as she drove, "not a lifetime, for crying out loud."

But those six years had brought about plenty of changes in her. She was taller, her hair was longer and blonder, plenty of visits to the orthodontist had made her teeth straighter, and her body had curves it had not possessed the last time she was in Dinsmore.

This was Erika's first trip back to the town since she'd left six years ago, and a flood of memories rushed through her as she drove leisurely up and down its streets, from the middle of town to her old house, then to her friends' old houses. When she found Karin's house, she slowed down, almost to a stop. It looked run-down and uncared for; the yard was overgrown, and the paint was peeling off the shutters. It looked abandoned, but Erika knew that couldn't be true. She'd been calling Karin for months before the date of their meeting—they'd all been trying to reach her, in fact—but only got the answering machine with Karin's mother's voice on it. None of the calls had ever been returned. She considered going to the door to see if anyone answered, but thought better of it. She'd wait till the others arrived.

24

Erika felt her stomach growl. She'd been traveling since very early that morning, and she hadn't eaten since breakfast. She drove by her old school, smiling, and decided to drop by a familiar hangout.

The last time Erika had been in the Burger Barrel was for lunch with her mother just days before they'd left, and the only thing that was different was the selection on the jukebox. The place was still the teenage hangout it had been back then, and the only adult she could see in the restaurant was a very thin, wrinkled woman with frizzy white hair who looked to be in her fifties standing behind the cash register, a half-smoked cigarette hanging from her rubbery lips. When she saw Erika seating herself in a booth, the woman put her cigarette in an ashtray and came to the table.

"Would you like coffee? A menu?" she asked in a horrible raspy voice.

Erika asked for coffee and a cheeseburger, trying not to wrinkle her nose at the waitress's smoke-ravaged voice.

As she waited for her order and sipped coffee, Erika wondered who would show up next. The girls had stayed in touch over the past six years—although they had not seen one another during that time—and all of them were coming that day. Except, of course, for Karin.

Their last encounter with Karin in the Waxhouse had remained vivid in Erika's mind. No matter how hard she tried to forget Karin's tearful, accusing voice crying out at them, she failed. And the memory always stirred in her feelings she fought to ignore.

What had been wrong with Karin? If, indeed, she had been suffering from some sort of mental illness, as the girls had suspected, perhaps it had progressed so much that she was no longer in any condition to see anyone. But if that was the case, what *kind* of mental illness had afflicted her? And the question that continued to haunt Erika: Could her illness have been worsened by the things Erika had said to her on one spring day?

She sighed and shook her head.

Erika's parents hadn't been crazy about the idea of her coming to Dinsmore by herself. She'd been telling them about the proposed meeting for years, reminding them it was a pact that she couldn't break, and they'd never seemed to mind the idea. But when the time finally came, they were shocked that she was actually considering traveling across the state by herself. When they finally realized she was *very* serious about the trip, her father set it up for her, trying to make it as safe as possible. He arranged the flight and the rental car, had even called ahead to reserve a motel room for her in Dinsmore. But he didn't have to pay for it, because Erika had been saving money for some time, and now had a job at a pet store in Santa Monica, which had provided the rest of the funds she needed. She smiled when she remembered her father's last words to her at the airport: "Don't talk to any strangers, and call us as soon as you get there." Still smiling, she went to the pay phone by the restrooms and called her parents collect to assure them that she was fine. Then she returned to her table.

Erika's cheeseburger came, and she took a big bite, realizing suddenly just how hungry she was. As she ate, the bell over the door clanged. Footsteps sounded on the tile floor, then stopped. Erika was aware of someone standing beside her booth.

"Erika?"

She looked up and dropped her burger onto the plate, where it fell to pieces. She moved out of the booth, shot to her feet, opened her arms wide, and shrieked, *"Bret!"* with a full mouth.

Heads turned and people stared as the girls embraced, laughing and jumping up and down. When they finished, they slid into the booth, but continued to hold hands over the table and leaned close, talking over one another with, "How *are* you," and, "You look *fantastic*!" and, "It's so good to *see* you!"

Eventually they stopped and simply stared at one another, grinning.

"You want something to eat?" Erika asked.

"Oh, no. I came in here to sit and listen to all the chewing."

She rolled her eyes. Bret hadn't changed; she still had a smart mouth.

Bret ordered a hamburger, and Erika reassembled her own. As they ate, they caught up.

"Your mom didn't mind your coming?" Erika asked.

"Oh, no, she doesn't mind anything. I can do anything I want as long as I don't get married."

"Married?"

"Yeah, she's afraid I'm going to turn out like her because she *knows* I'll marry the first guy who comes along just so I can get rid of the name Woinowski."

"So she's still single, huh?"

"She will *always* be single."

"How about you?"

Bret shrugged. "We'll talk about me later. How about *you*?"

Erika cocked a brow and smirked. "Oh, I've been kind of seeing somebody. Sort of."

"You've been *kind* of seeing him *sort* of? Well, either he's really short or your going blind. Which is it?"

"I told you about him in my last letter, doof. His name's Rick, and we've been going out pretty steadily for most of the summer."

"You should've brought him."

"Uh-uh. This is just for us girls."

A slight frown darkened Bret's eyes. "Yeah. That's what *I* said, but it didn't work."

"That's what you said to who?"

Bret took in a breath, let it out slowly. "His

28

name's Greg. I guess he's the guy my mom's afraid I'll marry.''

''Why? What's wrong with him?''

''Well, that depends on what you mean: what's wrong with him in real life, or what's wrong with him in my mom's eyes? I suppose there are things wrong on both sides, but usually what my mom sees is worst, and completely imaginary. As far as she's concerned, all males are suspicious and more than likely attend black masses and are cruel to small animals. But Greg's . . . well, he's not that bad.''

Erika leaned forward and asked cautiously, ''What do you mean, he's not *that* bad? How bad *is* he?''

Bret took a bite of her hamburger and didn't respond for a moment. When she finally spoke, she ignored Erika's question. ''He came with me.''

Erika looked around. ''Then where is he?''

''Outside. He said he was going over to the hardware store because . . . well—'' she chuckled humorlessly, ''he got pretty mad when I told him I didn't have a jack in the car, so he's going to try to find one. He's taking the car to Eureka while I'm here. He's got friends there.'' She spoke quietly with her head slightly bowed.

''You don't sound like you wanted him to come,'' Erika whispered.

Bret shrugged with one shoulder, a gesture of forced confidence, almost toughness. ''If he wants to go see his friends, that's fine. I just didn't think he'd have a good time with us. By the way, do you mind driving me around while he's gone?''

"Of course not,'' Erika said, but she wouldn't allow herself to be sidetracked. "Are you happy with this guy? Because . . . well, you don't sound too happy.''

Another shrug. "Greg has a temper, and everybody misunderstands him because of that. He gets it from his dad. Oh, his dad's awful. He beats up on Greg, even on Greg's mother. But Greg's not like that. I mean . . . well, he's not as bad as his dad.''

"Not *as bad*? What's that supposed to—'' She leaned forward even farther and hissed, "Bret, does this guy hit you or—''

"I got a jack,'' a rough voice said.

Erika looked up to see a guy she immediately assumed was Greg. He was tall and thin, wore an old, worn-out black leather jacket over a black Megadeth T-shirt, and faded blue jeans. His black hair was full and ended on his shoulders. He sniffed a lot. His narrow face looked as if it couldn't possibly smile.

Bret smiled up at him and tugged on his sleeve, trying to pull him into the booth beside her, saying, "Come here.''

He jerked his hand away, and his lip curled up. "I don't *want* to sit down. I want the keys.''

Bret sounded nervous when she introduced

30

them. As she searched her purse for the keys, Greg looked down at Erika and smiled at her. But it wasn't a friendly, nice-to-meet-you smile. His eyes moved over her like small, dirty hands, and he nodded his head ever so slightly, as if to let her know that he approved and wouldn't mind being alone with her sometime. The smile disappeared quickly, and he scowled down at Bret.

"Come on, *come on*!" he barked, snapping his fingers. "What'd you do, *bury* them in there?"

"Here they are, right here," Bret said, handing them to him as if he hadn't spoken to her that way, as if he hadn't growled at her like a disgruntled employer.

He took the keys in a fist. "So I'll meet you here tomorrow? Noon?"

"Yes." Then she turned to Erika. "If you don't mind bringing me here."

"Sure."

Greg leaned forward, slipped an arm beneath Bret's jacket and planted a kiss on her mouth hard. Erika averted her eyes; it was an embarrassing public kiss, not to mention what he was doing beneath Bret's jacket.

Bret made a small sound of protest and tried to pull away, but Greg's arm tensed, and he did something under the jacket that made Bret wince and swallow a pained yelp.

"Hey," he said very quietly, "remember

what we were talking about in the car a while ago? Huh?''

She nodded.

He finished the long, lewd kiss, then pulled away and whispered, ''Now, that was nice, wasn't it?''

After a moment she nodded.

Greg stood, nodded silently at Erika, then left the restaurant.

As Bret continued to eat, Erika stared at her in horror. Then, with great caution, she said, ''Um, look, Bret, you know, this is probably none of my business, but we're, you know, friends, and I don't think I could stand myself if I didn't tell you right now, *honestly*, that that guy is—''

Bret stared at her looking irritated, and said quietly, ''We're supposed to meet them at three, right?''

With her mouth open Erika frowned and nodded.

''Then we'd better hurry. It's getting late.''

Erika leaned back and watched Bret eat for a moment, then decided that any discussion of whatever had passed beneath the surface of their conversation earlier or any discussion about Greg would have to wait, because Bret obviously didn't want to talk about it now. With a sigh Erika continued to eat. When they were done, they paid their bill and rattled the bell over the door on their way out.

A light rain was still falling, but the girls

hardly noticed. Erika was still quite preoccupied with Bret's unsavory boyfriend (at least he seemed unsavory to her—apparently Bret saw him differently), and Bret was preoccupied with thoughts of her own. Erika stopped at the car, opened her purse, and began looking for her keys. She lifted her head to speak to Bret—just small talk to break the brittle silence between them—and saw Bret staring at something, staring with her lips parted and jaw slack, a half-smirk on her open mouth.

Erika turned around to see what Bret was looking at and saw Mrs. Potter, Karin's mother, walking quickly and stiffly down the sidewalk, her head bent forward slightly against the rain, a small purse clutched tightly in one fist.

"Mrs. Potter?" Erika called.

The woman's feet scraped on the sidewalk as she stopped suddenly and spun around to face them.

She still looked very much the same. She stood tall and straight, almost rigidly so, but was no longer thin as she used to be; now her body was thick and blocky. She had always been imposing—mostly because of the scar— but now she appeared threatening, with her stern wrinkled face and dark eyes beneath brown and silver hair pulled back tight in a bun. Even the scar had grown worse; it was becoming puckered, developing tiny creases around the edges, so that it strongly resembled

33

a sutured, V-shaped incision. Karin had once said her mother had gotten the scar in a car accident. Looking at it now, at how it had not only remained vivid on Mrs. Potter's flesh but had gotten even uglier, Erika decided it must have been an awfully bad car accident.

Mrs. Potter stared at them for a long time through narrowed eyes.

Erika stepped forward and said, "Remember us? I'm Erika. Erika Bryson? And this is Bret Woinowski."

As always, Bret made a face at the sound of her last name being spoken.

Mrs. Potter stared.

"Don't you remember us? We're friends of Karin's."

Mrs. Potter's head nodded very slowly, and she said in a low, level voice, "I know who you are."

"Well . . . we're getting together today. All of us. And we've been trying to get in touch with Karin because we'd like her to come and—"

"I'm sorry," she interrupted Erika. Her voice was cold and flat.

Erika waited for her to continue, but she didn't. "Well, um . . . could you tell us how to reach Karin so we can—"

"No."

Once again Erika stopped and stared at the odd woman.

"You *can't* reach Karin," she said. "Karin is dead. She killed herself." A cold and unemotional smile curled across Mrs. Potter's face. "Seems she wasn't *pretty* enough." Then she turned and hurried away.

TWO

Karin

I t had stopped raining, but Erika's windshield wipers were still slapping back and forth. Erika stared dumbly through the windshield until Bret muttered, "Rain's stopped." Then she turned them off. After riding in silence for some time, Erika said, "She didn't have to run off so fast. She could have at least talked, and . . . well, you know . . . told us more . . ."

"Oh, I don't know," Bret whispered. "I think she was pretty . . . succinct."

They said nothing more for a while as Erika drove, but each of them was thinking about Karin.

* * *

Erika and Bret had been next door neighbors in Dinsmore for as long as they could remember. They shared playpens and attended one another's birthday parties. Their parents were friends and took turns baby-sitting for one another. So it was natural that Erika and Bret were best friends when they started school. They remained best friends and, over the next couple of years, met Lynda and Leslie. The four of them became inseparable. It wasn't until the end of their third-grade year that Karin joined them.

Actually they had met her before that. She had always been around, standing alone on the edge of the playground during recess, sitting quietly in the very back of the classroom. She was round and bland and clumsy; she didn't have very nice clothes, and she kept her head down most of the time. She was the one— there's at least one in every class, at every school—who was ridiculed by the boys and quietly avoided by the girls.

Erika and the girls were bothered by the way Karin was treated, but did not speak of it, not even to each other. Erika knew they were being like too many of their classmates in remaining silent simply because it wasn't *in* to stick up for Karin Potter, and it bothered her, made her angry with herself. She didn't know it at the time, but Bret, Lynda, and Leslie felt the same.

One day they did something about it. They

spotted Karin on the playground during lunch-time surrounded by four cackling boys. They watched as the boys tossed the brown paper bag that contained Karin's lunch back and forth over her head and just out of her reach. The boys laughed and hooted as Karin jumped awkwardly for the bag, missing each time.

"You don't need lunch!" one of the boys shouted.

"You're too fat already!" another said.

"You need a diet!" still another called as Karin threw herself back and forth, up and down, trying to get her lunch back.

The girls watched for a few moments. Erika felt a knot tighten in her stomach, and her teeth clenched together as she listened to the boys' cruel laughter and remarks. Finally, unable to bear the scene any longer, she stalked across the playground toward them.

The other girls followed her, equally upset.

Erika stopped a couple of feet away from the boys, watching the bag being tossed back and forth, and waited until it landed in the hands of the boy directly in front of her, and then—

She jumped on him, wrapping her arms around his neck and her legs around his waist. The boy let loose a surprised yelp.

"Give it to her!" Erika shrieked. "Give her the lunch!"

The boy dropped the lunch as he staggered back and forth with Erika on his back. When another boy picked up the lunch and kept it from Karin, Bret rushed him, knocked him to the ground, and retrieved the bag herself.

For a brief moment a brawl broke out on the playground between the four girls and four boys. It stopped suddenly when Mrs. Donesky, their teacher, shouted, "Stop that right now!"

Mrs. Donesky gave them a lecture and especially scolded the boys for behaving that way with girls, then she made all of them spend the rest of the lunch period in the classroom, even Karin. The boys and girls sat on opposite ends of the room.

Karin said nothing to the girls at first, didn't even look at them. But when she finally lifted her eyes, a smile slowly spread across her face. "Thanks," she whispered.

As the girls talked and ate their lunches, Karin began to loosen up. Erika and her friends were surprised that Karin was fun to talk to, that she had a sense of humor. She really wasn't very different from anyone else. She was just overweight and shy, and everyone punished her for that day after day.

But now that Karin was part of the girls' clique, she was protected. Even though the other kids still talked about her among themselves, at least they had backed off her. Karin didn't think too much about *why* Erika, Leslie, Bret, and Lynda accepted her; she just was happy to finally have some friends.

Karin spoke of her mother rarely, her father

not at all. At first the girls thought it odd, but they didn't want to question or push Karin too much. Even though she'd opened up a lot, she still had a fragile, almost frightened, personality. One afternoon after hanging out in the park, the girls walked Karin home. She lived on the eastern edge of town, where the houses were smaller, older, and in poor condition, where dirty children played with broken toys on dead lawns. Mrs. Potter came out to meet them.

She was skinny, and her hair was bunched up beneath a blue scarf. She folded her arms and positioned her lips into something that could have been either a smile or a silent reprimand. Karin introduced her friends.

The girls said hello quietly and tried very hard not to stare at the garish, strawberry-colored scar on Mrs. Potter's face. Then she *did* smile, nodded her head once, said, "Pleased." She took Karin's hand and said, "Let's go inside now."

Mrs. Potter seemed a bit unpleasant, but the girls thought nothing of it. Some time later they learned that Karin's father had been electrocuted while working on the wiring in their house. Bret asked Karin about him one day while they were sitting on a rocky cliff overlooking the ocean.

"It happened right in front of me," she whispered hoarsely without looking at them. "I . . . I watched him die."

Karin's words that day haunted them, but at least now they had a possible reason for why Karin seemed so disturbed emotionally. One spring day when Karin and Erika were alone, Karin seemed especially quiet and morose. Erika asked her what was wrong, and she didn't answer for a while. Then she suddenly turned to Erika and asked, "Why don't people like me?"

Why don't people like me? Thinking back on it now, it was a simple question that Erika could have answered in a number of ways. It was also a question that had bothered Erika ever since, because she was afraid she'd answered it the wrong way.

About a year after Karin had blurted that question to Erika, her behavior took a turn for the worse. She seemed to be growing more withdrawn, more timid, as if she were reverting to the silent, pathetic girl she had been when they'd met her. Sometimes when they got together after school, Karin would become very nervous and jumpy, even afraid, and would leave them suddenly, hurrying away without giving any excuse. Sometimes she burst into tears unexpectedly or giggled when nothing was funny, and sometimes she just stared silently at something no one else could see. Over time, when the girls agreed to get together at a specific place and time, Karin showed up less and less frequently. She even began to miss school.

They kept asking her what was wrong, but she always assured them she was fine.

Then her mother withdrew her from school. They never saw her anymore, and when they called, her mother always said she couldn't talk. Karin called Erika once, but said very little before ending the conversation abruptly.

The last time the girls had seen Karin, that day at the Waxhouse, she'd left after her outburst as suddenly as she'd come, before they could ask her how she had been or what she'd been doing.

And now she'd hurried away from them in a more permanent way. Now she was dead . . .

"Do you think we were good enough to her, Bret?" Erika asked quietly.

"What do you mean?"

She thought for a long moment, then shook her head. "I don't know."

They said nothing more until they arrived at the Waxhouse.

THREE

The Waxhouse

Lynda and Leslie were already standing in front of the Waxhouse having an animated conversation when Erika and Bret drove up. The two girls rushed to the car, and once Erika and Bret were out, all four girls hugged one another and exchanged loud greetings that echoed up and down the street.

Once they'd settled down, Leslie turned and gestured toward the Waxhouse. "Look what's happened," she said gloomily.

As they turned to the big house, Erika and Brett groaned with disappointment.

The green lawn was no longer grass but weeds. The rectangular sign in the front that had read THE WAXHOUSE was now weathered and faded, the letters hardly legible. The red-berried pyracantha that Mr. Wattenberg had kept well trimmed alongside the porch was now growing wildly, crawling in all directions over the house's front wall, creeping toward the door as if it were trying to sneak inside. Paint peeled from the walls like old dried skin. But worst of all, the lower windows were all boarded up. It looked as if the house had died and was now decomposing.

"What happened?" Leslie asked, staring up at the boards that covered the windows on the top floors as well as the bottom.

"Do you think they died?" Lynda asked.

Bret said, "They were old enough."

Erika flinched and glared at her.

"Well, it's *true*, isn't it?" Bret asked defensively. "It's not like I'm saying something *bad* about them. They were *old*."

Erika whispered, "Well, you don't have to . . . you know, *say* it."

"Well, they're not going to hear us," Bret said, "because I've got a feeling they're not home."

The girls stopped suddenly and glanced at each other silently, then broke into laughter at their behavior. It was as if no time at all had passed between them, though their laughter was sad because of their discovery.

Changes had taken place across the street, too. Broussard's Market was gone; now only half of the sign remained, reading, MARKET. The windows looked grimy, and the building was dirty and in need of a paint job; the entire structure appeared to sag beneath its own weight. But it was still doing business. A car was parked at the gas pumps as a man filled his tank. A handwritten sign in one of the dirty windows advertised a sale on soda. Another read, COLD BEER.

Erika returned to her car and leaned against it with a sigh. Her shoulders sagged as she stared up at the old house with sad eyes. "Well," she whispered, shaking her head, "this is just too much."

"What do you mean?" Lynda asked with her usual bright smile. "You didn't expect things to be exactly as they were, did you? The important thing is that we're together. Right?"

Erika just stared silently at the house.

"Right?" Lynda repeated.

Bret stepped forward and said, "That's not the only thing she's talking about, Lynda." She bowed her head a moment, choosing her words. "Karin's dead," she blurted.

Lynda and Leslie froze, staring at Bret. Lynda's smile began to melt away slowly. Leslie swayed a bit, looking stunned.

"Karin Potter?" Lynda whispered.

Bret nodded, and quickly told her about their encounter with Mrs. Potter.

Leslie went to Erika's car and leaned against it next to her.

The joyful spell of their reunion was broken. They were suddenly a gloomier group of girls than they had ever been on their worst days together as children. They were silent for a long time until Lynda spoke up.

"Then we have to go see Mrs. Potter," she said with confidence. "We have to talk to her about Karin and find out what happened."

"I don't think she'll speak to us," Erika said. "Judging from the way she stalked away from us, I don't think she wants to talk to *any*-one."

"She'll understand," Lynda said. "We were Karin's friends. I think Mrs. Potter will understand that we want to know about her death. She'll invite us in, and we'll talk."

"I think Mrs. Potter's a little loopy," Bret said.

The others turned to her and waited for her to continue.

"Well, I mean . . . she's always been a little odd, I guess, but . . . well, after seeing her today, I think maybe Karin's death—Karin's *suicide*—hit her really hard and maybe pushed her over the edge." She turned to Erika. "What do you think?"

Erika considered it, then nodded. "Yeah, I think you may be right. I think we should probably leave Mrs. Potter alone. Sure, she was odd, but look what she's been through . . . first her husband, then her daughter. We can find out about Karin some other way. We could probably ask somebody here in town. There have got to be some people we knew still around. It wasn't *that* long ago."

They all nodded in agreement, then Lynda smiled and said, "Well, how about some lunch?"

"Bret and I have already eaten, but we'll go with you," Erika said.

"I'd like to go get my motel room first," Leslie said. "I feel gross, and I'd like to clean up."

"Yeah, that sounds good," Erika said. She turned to Bret. "Do you have a room?"

Bret was staring at the Waxhouse. "No. Not yet."

"Well, why don't you stay in mine?"

Bret continued to stare, then smirked as she slipped her fingers into the back pockets of her jeans.

"What's the matter?" Erika asked.

Bret turned to them and said, "I think we should stay here."

They gawked at her for a moment, then Erika said, "What?"

"I think we should stay in the Waxhouse. I mean—" She shrugged, grinning. "It's free, right? And it's not like we'll be imposing on anybody. I think it would be fun."

The girls just stared at her.

"Oh, come *on*, you guys!" she continued. "You haven't gotten *that* old in six years, have you? You even said, Erika, that you wanted us to meet here, at the Waxhouse. Well, let's *stay* here, too. I mean, what's the point of a reunion if we go off to separate, impersonal motel rooms?''

"I've got nice clothes with me," Leslie protested. "Do you know how filthy it must be in there?''

"Oh, it can't be that bad," Bret went on. "It'll be like camping. Remember that time we went camping together? Your dad took us, Erika, and we had a *great* time, didn't we? Well, it'll be like that.''

"I agree!" Lynda said enthusiastically. "Why get together if we're not going to do something special, something exciting? Why not make it something we'll remember? It'll be an adventure!''

"Sure," Erika said. "We'll remember being carted off by the police for breaking and entering.''

Leslie frowned. "And I'll *always* remember it if I go home with a bunch of ruined clothes.''

"Leslie, you've probably got so many clothes at home, you could never wear them all in your lifetime." Bret laughed, turning to Erika. "And *you*, you're starting to sound like *me*.''

Leslie asked, "Well, how will we get in? The windows are boarded, and I'm sure the doors are locked.''

"We'll break in," Bret replied.

Erika muttered, "You are scary, Bret.''

"Well?" Bret said. "How about it? You want to spend our reunion in our favorite place?

We'll get cookies and chips and lots of drinks. It'll be *fun*, you guys.''

Lynda nodded frantically.

Leslie said, ''Look, I wouldn't mind breaking in there for a while, maybe. But I am *not* going to sleep on a hard, cold floor.''

''Me, neither,'' Erika said. ''Anyway, I don't think it would be safe.''

Bret sighed. ''Well . . . okay. But why don't we buy some munchies and go inside for a while? Okay?''

Still worried about her brand-new outfit, Leslie nodded halfheartedly.

Finally Erika smiled at Bret and said, ''Yeah, that would be fun. But if we get in trouble, *you're* going to pay the bail.''

A pair of eyes watched them.

The eyes watched and a pair of ears listened as the girls talked about how they were going to break into the Waxhouse.

FOUR

Break-in

They went to the Seaview Motel, where Erika had a reservation, and Lynda and Leslie decided to share a room. The girls changed clothes and washed up. Bret took her Walkman and minispeakers from her bag and grabbed a few tapes. Lynda took the extra blankets from both of the rooms. "At least we don't have to sit on the dirty floor," she said.

Once they'd cleaned off the residue of travel, they returned to the Waxhouse. In spite of Leslie's protests that the store was too dirty, they decided to buy groceries at what used to be Broussard's Market, just for old time's sake.

In the shadowy gray glare of the rainy day, the lights of Broussard's glowed weakly. The gravel that had once covered the store's lot had thinned out, and little more than dirt remained, dirt that, in the rain, had become thick, doughy mud.

"See?" Leslie whined as she tiptoed through the mud. "I told you it was filthy here."

The door opened stiffly, and the girls were met with a cloying smell that made their noses wrinkle. It was slightly sweet, but at the same time slightly rancid, like fruit gone bad. And there was another odor woven in with the sour-sweetness: body odor.

There was a stack of hand baskets by the door, and Erika took one before walking deeper into the store. It was not as bright inside as she remembered it being, and the aisles seemed narrower, almost claustrophobic.

"So," Erika said quietly, "what do you want?"

They all spoke quietly as they decided on junk food and drinks, as if they didn't want anyone to hear them, to know they'd come in. As far as they could tell, they were the only customers in the store. They ambled down an aisle of canned goods as they discussed what to buy, then rounded the corner at the end and started down another aisle. Suddenly they all stopped.

A young man stood grinning at them in the center of the aisle. He looked like a stick figure drawn by a child except for the clothes he wore: old stained jeans, a tattered denim jacket over a dirty plaid shirt. His straw-color hair was uncombed and seemed to point or wave in every direction. He didn't have much of a chin, and his left eye was opened wider than his right. His skin appeared splotchy, which could have been its coloration or simply dirt and grime. One of his upper teeth stuck out on the left side of his mouth so that, even when his mouth was closed, part of it poked between his lips. He stood in such a way that made him seem to lean toward them, as if he were about to take a step, or maybe walk right up to them.

"You live around here?" he asked.

None of them responded at first. Then Erika said, "We used to."

He smiled around crooked yellow teeth. "But you don't now, huh?"

Erika shook her head slowly.

"Just visiting, huh?"

The girls all nodded.

He took a step forward, then another, closer, until he was just inches from Erika and Bret. His mud-color eyes darted back and forth between them as he asked quietly through his lopsided grin, "You want me to help you find something?"

Erika backed away from him a step, trying, out of politeness, not to look like she was cringing.

"Leo!" a deep voice barked behind them from the direction of the register. "You leave them lovely young ladies alone. Go find your brother. He was supposed to bring me another box of them paper towels.''

Leo flinched and backed away from them quickly. ''Yes, Daddy,'' he called. A moment ago he'd seemed to be somewhere in his twenties; suddenly he looked like a frightened boy of fourteen. Leo hurried around them, went behind the counter and through the door behind it.

The girls stared at one another silently a moment, mouths open, their eyes saying, *Did that guy just happen to us or what?* Then they went about their business, choosing bags of chips, tins of dips, a few bags of chocolate chip cookies. As they shopped, they heard a soft rolling sound over the wood floor, then that deep voice again: ''You young ladies visiting our fine little town?''

They all spun around to see an enormous froglike man hunched forward in a wheelchair. He was balding, with a few tufts of thin greasy hair around his crown. His big nose was flat, as if it had been smashed against his face, and when he smiled at them, he showed only a few remaining stained teeth.

''Um, yes, we're visiting,'' Erika said, trying to keep her voice from trembling when she saw that he was wheeling even closer to them, moving too fast for her comfort. ''But we used to live here in Dinsmore.''

He stopped suddenly, looking up at them through squinty eyes. ''Well, that's too bad.

Wish you *still* lived here. This town needs more fine young ladies like yourselves. I've got two sons, and around here they don't seem to have much choice in who they keep company with.''

"Well," Bret said, her voice level and final, "I'm sure they'll find someone." She turned to the others. "What would you like to drink?"

"Got a sale on soda," the man said.

"Yeah, soda sounds good," Lynda said. "Diet, of course."

Leslie added, "I don't want any caffeine."

As if they were one person, the girls turned away from the man and headed for the cooler of soft drinks against the wall behind them. They were talking among themselves, trying to ignore the man in the wheelchair, when they heard footsteps coming from the direction of the counter.

"Here's them paper towels, Dad," another voice said, and a box thunked down on the counter.

Erika and the others turned to see another young man, a little older than the first, wearing a dirty blue jumpsuit and an unwashed pea green jacket. He was tall but pudgy, with short hair that was so uneven and choppy, it looked as if he'd cut it himself. Erika noticed that the edges of his fingernails were dark with dirt. She saw the man in the wheelchair—who had wheeled back over to the counter—nod toward the girls, and the young man turned to them.

"Got some visitors, Jerry," the man said. "Girls from out of town. Say they used to live here."

Jerry nodded his acknowledgment, but continued to stare at the girls silently, expressionlessly, until one corner of his thin-lipped mouth curled up in a smirk that looked neither friendly nor wholesome.

Hoping the others would follow her example, Erika turned to the cooler and went back to choosing soft drinks.

"Can you be*lieve* these freaks?" Bret whispered.

"Sh!" Leslie hissed. "Let's talk about them later."

"Right," Erika whispered. "Let's just get out of here."

They headed for the register, and on the way stopped to grab some flashlights—there were only three—and batteries. The man in the wheelchair was behind the counter, ready to ring up their purchases. Jerry, on the other hand, stood on their side of the counter, meaty arms folded over his meaty chest, watching them closely as they approached. His eyes moved from one to the other of them; his smirk grew into an oily, malignant smile as they neared.

They walked around Jerry and kept their distance as Erika emptied the hand basket onto the counter. They fished cash out of their purses and wallets and assembled the total as the man in the wheelchair bagged their groceries.

Jerry simply watched them, smiling, running the tip of his tongue over his lips now and then. Finally he reached out and ran a finger over Lynda's hair and said, "You doing anything tonight?"

She jerked her head away and turned away from him.

"Thank you," Erika said, taking one bag while Bret took the other. They turned and hurried for the door.

Jerry said, "How about you?" as he reached out and brushed his fingertips over Bret's behind.

She nearly dropped the bag as she swung around and slapped his arm so hard that a *crack* resounded through the store. The others gasped.

Jerry pulled back, and his face opened in an expression of shock and silent anger that was so cold, it frightened Bret for a moment. Then she turned and headed for the door with the others.

Leo suddenly stepped out from behind a display case of Hostess pies and stopped in front of them, making them stumble to a halt.

"You shouldn't be so impolite," he said quietly, looking them over with lewd and shifty eyes. "My brother was just trying to be friendly."

"Excuse us," Erika said firmly in spite of her

fear. She stepped around him, and the others followed.

They didn't even notice the mud this time, taking long and rapid steps across it, not even bothering to avoid puddles. They were all trembling. They'd almost reached the road when Bret released a quiet, breathy sound of anger.

"Can you believe that?" she hissed, then stopped and looked over her shoulder toward the store. When she didn't start walking again, they all stopped and looked back.

Leo and Jerry stood in front of the store. Leo shifted his weight back and forth from foot to foot; Jerry remained perfectly still. Their eyes were pools of shadow beneath furrowed brows, and their lips were pressed tightly, angrily together.

"Come on, let's just go," Erika said, her voice trembling slightly.

"Look, maybe we shouldn't stick around now," Leslie said. "I mean, after *that* . . . you know?"

"Hell, no," Bret growled. "I'm not going to let some inbred freaks spoil our day." She was actually stomping her feet as they crossed the street to the Waxhouse.

Casually each of them glanced back in turn.

Leo and Jerry were still there, watching them.

"Can you believe those guys?" Bret went on as they crossed the lawn. "Right out of *The*

Texas Chainsaw Massacre. They've probably got a deformed brother hidden in the back room wearing a leather hood over his head made of human skin.''

Lynda giggled as Leslie said, ''I think somebody held their heads under the gene pool a little too long.''

''It wasn't a gene pool,'' Erika replied, ''it was a gene *swamp*.''

Their laughter was a slight release from their tension, but it remained nervous laughter. Leo and Jerry had frightened them, and the fact that the two young men were so close did not allow them to shake off their fear.

''You know, maybe we *shouldn't* stick around,'' Erika said quietly once they'd reached the car. ''I mean, we can go back to the motel and have a good time. We can talk and pig out and—''

''If they wanted to, they could just follow us there,'' Bret said, glancing back at the store. They were still there. ''No. They'll leave us alone. They're a lot of wind and swagger, but I don't think they'll do anything.'' Her voice did not sound convincing, but the others went along with what she said.

After they put the groceries in the front seat of Erika's car, Erika looked up at the old house and said to Bret, ''Okay, it was your idea. So how do we get in there?''

Bret shrugged. ''I don't know.''

58

"You don't *know*?" the other three girls cried, almost simultaneously.

"But you *talked* like you knew!" Leslie said.

Erika added, "You talked like it was no big deal."

"It's not," Bret replied. "It's a boarded-up house, not an armored car. You see any armed guards? Besides—" She nodded out the window at the winter's early darkness that was closing in around them. "The darker it gets, the better. I don't think the place will be well lit."

"So?" Erika said.

"So we look around. Sometimes windows are left unlatched, that sort of thing."

"These windows are boarded *up*," Leslie said.

"Well, let's just *look*, okay?"

"Yeah, let's look." Lynda grinned. "I think it will be fun."

They loaded the flashlights with batteries and followed Bret's lead.

The night was taking over; a mist was crawling inland from the ocean as the last faint light of day—already darkened by the heavy rain clouds—began to fade away. Their footsteps sounded crisply on the cobblestone walk and up the steps. The wooden porch creaked beneath their weight more than it had the last time they'd been there.

"So we're just going to go in the front door?" Leslie asked.

"I don't know yet," Bret replied. She tried the door, but it wouldn't budge. In spite of the weathered appearance of the house, the lock was still in fine shape. "No," Bret said finally, "we're not going in the front door. Let's go around back."

"Why?" Erika asked.

"Because hardly anybody locks the bathroom window." She walked by them, went back down the steps and across the lawn, then around the corner of the house. The girls hurried after her.

"But these windows are boarded up," Erika remarked. "And it looks like they were boarded up pretty recently, too." She flicked on her flashlight and shined it at the boards that covered the windows. They looked rather new and sturdy and very firmly nailed onto the house.

"So, we'll do our best to tear some of those babies down, is all," Bret said with a smile.

"Um . . . Bret?" Lynda said hesitantly.

"What?"

"I, um . . . I don't like this all of a sudden."

"Why?"

"We're breaking in."

Bret laughed. "You expected an invitation?" She didn't slow down, just kept pushing down the strip of grass along the side of the house, between the wall and the pyracantha that had swallowed the fence surrounding the house, and the girls picked up their pace as she rounded the back corner. "Here it is," she said as the others came around after her.

The flashlight beam was shining on the small square window to the Wattenberg's first-floor bathroom. The windowsill was eye level to the girls. Unlike all the others around the house, it had only one board nailed across it, and it was warped enough to have loosened the rusty nail on the left. Bret stood on tiptoe beneath the window, reached up, and grabbed the board. The nail squeaked once and moved just a bit, but didn't come all the way out. She wedged the long, gray flashlight under the board and used it to pull out the nail. The board dropped down and swayed back and forth from its remaining nail like a creaky pendulum.

She turned to them and smiled, cocking the flashlight on her shoulder like a rifle. "See? That wasn't so hard."

"We aren't inside yet," Erika said with a smirk.

"No problem." Bret stood on tiptoe again and grunted as she tried hard to push up the sash. When it didn't work after several tries, she handed the flashlight to Lynda and used both hands. There was a small crunching sound, as if the sash were about to give way and slide up, but nothing happened.

"Maybe it's locked," Lynda offered timidly.

"*Nobody* locks the bathroom window," Bret insisted, trying again stubbornly.

"That's not a written law, is it?" Leslie

asked. "I mean, maybe *some* people *do* lock their bathroom windows."

"Besides," Erika added, "nobody lives here anymore, remember?"

Bret kept pushing, grunting with the effort, but in spite of an occasional creak or crunch, the window did not open.

"Flashlight," she said, holding out her hand. Lynda gave it to her, and she pressed the back end of it to the top of the sash and pushed. The light fell on her face, which was screwed up into a mask of exertion. She stopped.

"Give it up," Erika said.

Bret tried again, harder this time, and the flashlight slipped and hit the glass. There was a thick crack, the windowpane broke into three pieces and fell into the bathroom with a clatter, leaving behind a few jagged shards along the edges.

They stared silently at the window for a moment.

"We're all going to jail," Bret said quietly.

"Uh-uh, *you're* going to jail," Erika told her.

Leslie said, "Is this *exciting* enough for you, Lynda? *Adventurous* enough?"

"Everybody just calm down," Lynda said. "It's just a window, okay? How bad is that? It's not like we, you know, *killed* somebody."

"She's right," Bret said. Then she used the flashlight to knock the remaining shards out of the window. They clattered and cracked on the floor inside.

"What are you *doing*?" Erika hissed.

Bret reached up and unlatched the window, then pushed up the sash. After handing the flashlight to Lynda again, she gripped the bottom edge of the window and pulled herself up the wall and through the small opening.

"Careful of the glass on the floor," Lynda said.

Bret paused, her legs hanging out the window. They heard her scraping glass out of the way. Then she slid out of sight and thunked to the floor. A moment later her face appeared, and she grinned out at them and laughed. "Come on in!"

FIVE

Inside

As they had expected, it was dark, but it was *much* darker than they had expected. A thick fog of impenetrable darkness swirled around them once they were inside. The three flashlights cut through it, but the darkness remained pressed against the borders of the light, waiting to rush in at them again at the first opportunity.

"How many batteries did we get, by the way?" Leslie asked.

"Enough," Erika replied.

"Are you sure?" Leslie pressed.

"Positive, because we're not staying in here long enough to use them up."

"Oh, come on." Bret laughed.

"This is silly, Bret. We can't see anything,

it's damp in here, and the place is probably full of . . . oh, I don't know, *rats*, maybe.''

''*Rats?*'' Lynda asked.

''Oh, you guys are wimps,'' Bret said. ''Who wants to go get the food?''

''Won't that attract the *rats*?'' Lynda hissed.

Bret said slowly, ''The only rats in Dinsmore are across the street in that market picking imaginary lint off their jumpsuits. The worst we'll find is a mouse or two. *Maybe*. So do I go get the food, or what?''

''Why don't you just wait till we've looked around a little,'' Erika suggested. ''In a few minutes *you* might not want to stick around, either.''

''I doubt it.'' Bret shouldered past them and led the way out of the bathroom.

A dank, musty smell clung to everything in the house, a smell that conjured images of emptiness and decay. Circles of light from the flashlights slid over the peeling walls of the hallway. Where once there hung pictures of the Wattenbergs' past, the stains of neglect spread over what remained of the old wallpaper.

Lynda gasped, and the rest of them stopped abruptly. She was shining her flashlight on an old sampler hanging on the wall. It read, GOD BLESS THIS HOME.

''I guess they didn't get everything,'' Leslie said.

They kept going, past the bedroom, through the kitchen and dining room and into the small

65

living room. Furniture hunkered in the darkness. The flashlight beams fell on dirty white sheets that conformed to the shapes of the sofa and chairs. Familiar braided rugs still lay on the floor where they'd always been, now worn and tattered. Drapes still hung over the windows.

"You think they died and everything was just . . . left here?" Lynda asked.

"Maybe," Erika replied, then crossed the room and went through the door that led into the first room of the Waxhouse. She turned around, lifting the flashlight so the beam swept over the walls, and—

She saw a pair of eyes, a face with an open mouth, a body with arms spread wide above her as it threw itself down toward her.

Erika screamed and dropped her flashlight, stumbling backward until she fell. The flashlight rolled back and forth over the floor, and its light washed over the feet of the other girls as they rushed toward Erika.

"It's okay, it's okay," Lynda babbled, kneeling beside her.

Bret said, "Look, Erika, look." She lifted her flashlight. "Look, it's just one of the wax figures, that's all. That's all."

Erika's eyes followed the beam of light all the way up to the face of Jesus Christ. The wax was now covered with a gummy film of dust that distorted the features of the face. Her rapid heartbeat, brought on by fear, began to slow down, and she took a deep breath as she sat up.

"Sorry about that," she said. "It just looked scary in the dark. And I didn't expect to see it."

"I wonder why they're still here," Lynda mused, shining her light on the other figures in the room.

Bret helped Erika to her feet and said, "Maybe they didn't want to leave and decided to rent the place."

"Very funny." Erika chuckled as she picked up her flashlight.

"Why am I the only one here who doesn't have a flashlight?" Leslie asked.

"Because we only bought three, and you were the last one to reach into the bag," Bret replied. "Why?"

"Well, because . . . I don't like the . . . well, I'd just *like* one, that's all."

"Because of them?" Erika asked, nodding toward the figures.

Leslie became defensive. "I suppose you think they're amusing?"

"They're just wax," Bret replied. "Look. There's Napoleon. He's not scary. Just short. And Joan of Arc. What's wrong with her? Of course, Genghis Khan is a little nightmarish, but he's *wax*."

"It's not that. It's just that they're . . . *here*. In the dark."

"I agree," Lynda said. "Let's go. We can eat in the motel."

"You guys are such *wusses*!" Bret remarked.

"Well, it is pretty creepy, Bret," Erika said.

"That's what makes it fun! Look, I'll go get the food. And when I get back, you can have my flashlight, Leslie."

Erika said, "I don't know, Bret . . ."

"Oh, come on, let's get this show on the road. The soda's getting warm out in the car, and besides . . . we've got a lot of catching up to do."

Bret grinned like a schoolgirl, and it made the rest of them do the same. They *did* have a lot of catching up to do, and none of them could think of a more appropriate place to do it. Yes, it was cold and damp and dark . . . but it was the Waxhouse, *their* Waxhouse.

"Okay," Erika said, smiling.

"I'll come help," Leslie volunteered, following Bret out.

Lynda called after them, "And don't forget those blankets!" Then she turned to Erika and said, "I think this will be fun."

Somewhere, ears listened to the tense voices . . . the footsteps . . . the scream . . . Then the tension drained from the voices, and they became more relaxed, more jovial.

They were settling in.

They had decided to stay.

SIX

Noises in the Dark

The Fantasy room filled with the sound of crunching.

"I think the ranch-flavored chips are best," Lynda said.

"Uh-uh," Bret argued. "Nacho cheese."

"Those don't come *close* to these Hawaiian chips," Leslie said.

Erika wrinkled her nose. "But those are so *greasy*."

They went on like that for a while, arguing about which junk food was best, that some were healthier than others.

They had spread their blankets in the middle of the room, surrounded by the grimy, shadowy figures of fairy tales, and positioned their flashlights so there was plenty of light between them, if not much around them.

The figures loomed over them in every direction, most of them cute and whimsical in good light, but exactly the opposite in such gloomy darkness.

Little Red Riding Hood's dusty face was open in a silent scream as the enormous wolf closed in on her, his yellowed fangs showing through a malicious grin beneath sinister golden eyes.

Jack Horner sat in the corner with a damaged pie in his lap; grinning, he held up his thumb, on the end of which rested a big, sloppy plumb. But in the murky glow of the flashlights, there was nothing pleasant about the little boy's toothy grin—with small teeth now darkened by dust—and the lumpy glob on the end of his thumb looked more like something viscous and disgusting than a simple plumb.

Little Miss Muffet ate from her bowl as a large, hairy spider—made to look even more realistic by all the authentic cobwebs that clung to everything around it—made its way down a web over her. In the girls' shifting shadows, the spider appeared, every now and then, to move.

Alice chased the White Rabbit; and Bilbo Baggins, the hairy-footed little hobbit, walked beside Gandalf the wizard on their journey; but the worst of all was Humpty Dumpty. He wasn't sitting on the wall, he was just starting to fall from it with spindly arms splayed and mouth and eyes open wide in fear. But that fear became malevolence in the shadows, and the girls tried to ignore him up there on that wall, because it looked as if he were about to pounce on them, his arms spread to take them all in a smothering, permanent embrace.

It took a little time, but they finally started talking about themselves and each other.

"So, how's your dad doing, Leslie?" Erika asked.

Leslie shrugged and took a moment to answer. "He's doing pretty well," she said. "Better than I expected, to tell you the truth. We were all expecting my mother's death, but . . . when it finally happened . . ." She sighed and shook her head. "For some reason it made me look forward to this little reunion even more. It seemed like a good way to—" She gave a half-embarrassed shrug as her voice lowered slowly, almost to a whisper. "You know, go back to a time when we were all together, and Mom was alive and pretty healthy, and . . . and Dad looked a lot younger, and my brother wasn't so silent and . . . morose." She gave them a crooked smile. "I guess that's a lot to expect from a little get-together, huh?"

"Not at all," Lynda told her. "I mean, that's why we're doing this, right?"

Leslie nodded, then asked, "So how's life in New York, Lynda?"

"Well, we don't live in New York City, remember," Lynda replied. "We live in West-chester. But New York is close, so we can go there a lot, and we do, and it's *so* much fun! I saw *Cats* three times, and when we went to see *Phantom of the Opera*, Daddy took me backstage to meet Michael Crawford, and he gave me his autograph and *kissed* me. I mean, he just leaned over and *kissed* me, right on the cheek. I thought I would die!"

"Who's Michael Crawford?" Bret asked.

Lynda stared at her a moment, dumb-founded. "You don't know? He's a Broadway star!"

Bret said, "Look, I live in a tiny Oregon town. The only Broadway we've got there has a 7-Eleven, a Laundromat, a video store, and a dog grooming shop on it."

"How's school, Lynda?" Erika asked.

"Busy, but fun. Being student body president kept me running, but—"

"You were student body president last year?" Erika asked, surprised.

"Yes. I told you that in my letter."

"No you didn't! But you were a junior. That position's always held by seniors."

Lynda shrugged. It was no surprise. Even when they were little girls, she was constantly busy, involved in organizing something at school or something of her own devising. "Summer's been a nice break," she went on, "but I'll be back at it again after school starts. Unless I don't get reelected."

"I doubt that'll happen," Bret said with a smirk.

Lynda reached over and slapped Bret's knee. "Okay, now it's your turn."

"Oh, I've got nothing unusual to report. Same as always. I'm doing so-so in school, I get along so-so with my mother. I've got some friends I hang out with. One in particular." She looked down at her lap and was silent a moment. "His name is Greg." Then she popped a chip into her mouth.

"Ooh," Leslie said. "This is news. A boyfriend?"

"Well . . . sort of."

"Is he cute?" Lynda asked.

Bret turned slowly to Erika and said, "Well, what do you think, Erika? Is he cute?"

Erika flinched at the question. Was she going to have to be honest here?

Leslie turned to her and said, "You met him? Is he here?"

Bret said, "He came with me, but he went on to Eureka to see some friends." She paused, then said to Erika: "So what do you think? Is he cute?"

All eyes turned to her, and the girls waited for a response.

"Well . . . he's got nice . . ." She searched her memory for something that was nice about Greg—his eyes, his mouth, his hair—but everything about him had seemed . . . *wrong*. At

73

least, wrong for Bret. "He's got a few, you know, rough edges, but, um . . ."

"You don't like him," Bret said with a smirk.

Erika opened her mouth to protest, but stopped. How could she deny it? It was true. She did not like Greg, and she couldn't tell her friend otherwise. She closed her mouth and shook her head.

Bret nodded. "Don't worry. You're not the only one. Greg makes people nervous. Especially my mother. Of course, if you took a single male hormone and dropped it in a milk carton and handed it to her, her hair would stand on end, so *all* men make *her* nervous. But . . . yeah, I guess Greg's a little off-putting."

Leslie and Lynda were silent, looking back and forth from Erika to Bret. They sensed a sudden tension between them, although they didn't understand it.

Erika stared at Bret, debating her next words, then very quietly said, "He's more than that, Bret. He's kind of scary."

Bret ate some more chips, but didn't respond.

"Bret, you said Greg's dad beat up on him and his mom, and you said Greg wasn't *as bad* as his dad. What did that mean? Does he hit you?"

"Well . . . I really, um, don't want to get into it, but . . . yeah, he does get a little rough when he's upset. But—" A shrug. "I know how to handle him."

Lynda leaned forward. "Bret, why would you want to *be* with someone like that? I'm really surprised! You've always been so . . . well, so self-confident, so sure of yourself, so unwilling to take any crap from anybody. Why would you put up with *that*?"

Bret did not meet their eyes. She stared at her can of soda as she continued to munch on chips. Finally: "Yeah, I know what you're saying. And I don't like it, I really don't. But it's not that easy to . . . well, to break it off now."

"Have you tried?" Leslie asked.

"A couple of times." Bret's voice was almost a whisper. "First I just told him, the way you'd tell any guy you didn't want to see him anymore. I told him it just wasn't working, that we weren't really, you know, right for each other, and . . . he blew up. I mean, he just lost it."

"Did he hurt you?" Erika asked.

"Not . . . really."

Erika's eyes widened, and she took a breath to speak again, but decided not to pursue that point for the time being.

"So then," Bret went on, "I thought maybe I could *show* him I didn't want to be with him anymore. I started flirting with this guy named Sam. We went out once. Somehow Greg found out. He showed up while Sam and I were in an ice cream parlor. He leaned over the table and whispered to me, in this cold, scary voice, 'I'll get you for this. I don't know how, but you won't be expecting it. I'll get you back for this, I swear.' Later he acted as if it had never happened. And he didn't go away. It was business as usual.''

"Did he ever get back at you?" Leslie asked.

Bret swallowed and licked her lips before whispering, "Not yet."

"What are you going to do?" Lynda asked.

Bret shrugged. "Just keep trying until he gets the picture, I guess. I mean, what else can I do?" The others stared silently at Bret for a while, then Bret forced a laugh. "Come on, you guys, stop looking so glum. Let's talk about somebody else for a while, okay?"

Erika was uncomfortable with letting it drop, but decided she could talk more with Bret later. They continued to talk about guys, exploring the topic from every possible angle. Lynda told them about her ex-boyfriend who, after being dumped by the girl who had broken them up in the first place, wanted to get back together. Leslie said she wasn't dating anyone, but she talked in great detail about a couple of guys she'd had her eye on for a while.

As they talked and laughed, Erika became quiet, nibbling on potato chips now and then, sipping a soda. Her mind drifted slowly from the topic at hand and settled elsewhere.

"So, Erika," Bret said, tugging on Erika's arm, "tell us about this guy of yours."

She blinked several times as she lifted her head and looked at them. "What? Oh, um . . . I'm sorry, I . . . wasn't listening."

"What's wrong?" Lynda asked.

Erika took in a deep breath and let it out slowly. "I was thinking about Karin."

The room became quiet.

"I wish she were here," Erika went on. "If I'd known she wasn't going to be, if I'd known she was . . . going to *kill* herself . . . I would have said more the last time we saw her. I would have . . . I would have . . . oh, I don't know *what* I would have done."

"What you said to her that day was wonderful, Erika," Lynda said. "She was really upset, but you made her feel better. You calmed her down."

"Why do you suppose she said those things about us?" Leslie asked.

Lynda shrugged.

Erika said, "Do you think she really thought those things?"

"Of course she did," Bret answered. "And . . . in a way . . . they were true."

The girls turned to her in shock.

"*What?*" Erika gasped. "We didn't hate her! At least *I* didn't."

"Oh, no," Bret replied. "Of course we didn't hate her. But the other things she said . . . about us talking about her behind her back . . ."

All of them averted their eyes like guilty children.

"That only happened once," Lynda said. "And we all felt bad about it."

"But we *did* it," Bret said. "We *all* did it. I'm just as guilty. We all did our impressions of Karin. The way she walked and talked, the way her hair was always fixed. We made fun of her. We did exactly what she accused us of doing the last time we saw her."

It had happened at a slumber party at Bret's house. Karin had been invited, but was unable to come. Late that night, in Bret's room, the girls began to imitate Karin. None of them could remember now how it had started, but once it had, they'd gotten carried away. They'd mimicked her chubby, uncoordinated walk, her timid way of speaking; they'd taken clothes from Bret's closet and mismatched them to mock her way of dressing, and they'd wet their hair to make it stringy or put it up in clumsy, sagging buns to imitate the way she did her hair. They'd gone on until Erika had stopped and reminded them—and herself—how others had treated Karin before they'd met her, how shy and withdrawn she'd been before she'd started hanging out with them. "We mean a lot to Karin," Erika had said, "and she's our friend. This is wrong. We shouldn't be doing it." They had stopped, and they hadn't done it again.

Erika frowned. "You don't think she might have found out about that, do you? I mean, none of us told her about it . . . right?"

They all nodded firmly.

"That was just how she felt," Erika said. "She didn't have a very high opinion of herself, so naturally she would think everyone else felt the same."

"But don't you think we kind of pitied her?" Bret asked.

"Of course we did," Lynda replied. "It was awful the way people treated her."

"But were we really any better? Were we giving her better treatment by making her a charity case?"

"She wasn't a *charity* case!" Leslie said defensively. "She was a nice girl. We all liked her. At least *I* did."

"Sure we liked her," Bret said. "But, Leslie, when you and I became friends, was it because you felt sorry for me?"

"Well . . . no."

"That's what I mean. We liked her once we got to know her. But maybe we got to know her for the wrong reasons."

"What difference does it make *why* we got to know her?" Lynda asked.

Bret sighed. "All I'm saying is maybe Karin was right when she said she was our pet charity."

"I don't agree," Leslie said. "I think we were—"

She stopped abruptly when they heard a sound from somewhere deep in the house. It was a small sound, not very loud, but unexpected and startling.

The girls froze, their eyes darting around, scanning the menacing figures that lurked in the dark all around them.

"What was that?" Lynda breathed.

"Sounded as if it came from somewhere up there." Leslie lifted her eyes slowly toward the ceiling.

"I think it's just the house," Bret whispered. "You know, settling. There was a breeze coming up when we went outside for the food. Maybe it's getting windy."

"It wasn't *that* much of a breeze," Leslie said.

Bret said, "I'm just saying that maybe it picked up and now it's—"

The sound came again, but this time it seemed to come from a different place.

"Okay, I'm leaving," Leslie declared, standing up.

"No, no, wait." Bret stood with her. "It's nothing. Let's look around, and I'll show you. There's nobody here."

"But what if somebody is?" Erika asked, standing with them. "I mean, what if some crazy person lives in here, or something?"

"How does he get in?" Bret asked. "We almost didn't. Come on, let's look around a little. I wanted to, anyway."

Lynda joined them as they followed Bret out of the Fantasy room and into Great Moments in History. Their beams swept back and forth through the darkness.

"See?" Bret said. "Nothing here." She led them across that room and into the room that used to hold the Wattenbergs' collection of American Leaders. But, as Mrs. Wattenberg had said, the room had been changed. Now their flashlights found the dust-covered faces of movie stars.

Marilyn Monroe's platinum blond hair was covered with cobwebs that dangled over her face like a veil. Clark Gable's arm had fallen off. In a scene from *Whatever Happened to Baby Jane?* Bette Davis glared threateningly at a wheelchair-bound Joan Crawford.

"They're all old stars," Bret complained. "There's nobody new."

"Yes, there is," Erika said. "Over here."

They turned to see her flashlight illuminating the face of Tom Cruise. He wore a silver jump-suit and carried a racing helmet under one arm. Beside him stood a figure of Robert Duvall.

"Right out of *Days of Thunder*," Erika said.

"Wow," Leslie whispered. "They did a great job."

Lynda said, with equal reverence, "Tom Cruise is so gorgeous."

"Think we can fit him in the car?" Bret asked.

They broke into laughter, but fell silent abruptly when they heard another sound.

"That one wasn't upstairs!" Leslie hissed.

"Maybe those creeps from the store are trying to get in," Lynda said. "Maybe they're after us!"

"It was just wood creaking," Bret assured her with a chuckle. "It's an old house, you have to expect a few noises. Come on, let's go upstairs."

"Okay, I get it." Erika folded her arms and turned to Bret.

"You get what?" Bret asked.

"What you're doing. It's a joke, right? A practical joke? You're setting us up for a scare, right?"

"Would you *chill*?" Bret laughed. "How could I do that? I haven't been here in six years, just like you."

"Then why do you keep hounding us to stay here, to look around, to go upstairs? How come you hounded us to come in here? It's just like before, when we were kids. You're doing it again, right?"

"Okay, okay. Look, you guys." Bret held up a hand, palm out, and closed her eyes. "If you want to go back to the motel and sit around in one of the rooms and watch a television with wobbly reception and smell that grody disinfectant motel room smell, that's fine. I just thought this would be more fun, okay? But if *you* guys want to go back, *fine.*"

— Erika didn't want to be a party pooper, and when she looked at the other two girls, she could tell they felt the same way. But she still didn't feel right about creeping around in the

82

old abandoned house. Even if the sounds they'd heard were nothing at all, simply being there felt wrong, intrusive and disrespectful to their old friends. Then again, Mr. and Mrs. Wattenberg probably wouldn't mind at all.

"All right," Erika said. "Let's go upstairs."

"Or," Bret said mischievously, "we could go down to the basement."

Leslie replied abruptly, "Yeah, you can *bite* that idea."

Laughing, they left the movie stars behind and headed up the stairs.

The carpet on the stairs was tattered and worn; holes had opened in the fabric, and flaps of the carpet had come loose, so the girls had to be careful not to trip on their way up. They moved slowly, carefully; occasionally a step would creak, making one of them flinch or utter a sharp little gasp.

"Boy, you guys really *are* wusses," Bret said, shaking her head as they reached the second-floor landing. "A step creaks, and you wet your pants. You're worse now than you were in the sixth grade."

"In the sixth grade," Erika replied, "we didn't know anything about serial killers."

"And none of us had read Stephen King," Leslie added.

Bret asked, "Want to go on up to the workroom?"

They headed up the next flight of stairs to

the attic. Erika opened the door. It moved stiffly, and she had to lean on it hard to get it all the way open. Once she'd succeeded, they walked in.

The door began to squeak shut behind Leslie, the last one in the room.

Flashlight beams moved over the once-cluttered worktables, over the old clothes hanging on the rack, encased in cobwebs, and—a rusted ax stuck in the middle of the wood floor beside a pile of amputated arms and legs.

The darkness filled with screams.

SEVEN

Locks

"**H**old it! *Hold* it!" Bret shouted. She'd screamed, too, but the others were *still* screaming, especially Lynda. When they stopped, their backs pressed against the door as they stared in horror at the pile of limbs. Bret said, "They're just wax. See?" She went to the pile, picked up a thin, feminine arm, and tapped it with the end of the flashlight to show that it was solid and artificial. "See?"

Erika stepped forward and took the arm, inspecting it with a frown.

"What're they doing piled in the middle of the floor?" Leslie asked as she and Lynda joined the girls.

"I think a better question," Erika said, "is

why there is an ax stuck in the middle of the floor.''

''Well, look how rusty it is,'' Bret said. ''It's probably been here for a long time.''

Erika asked, ''But why? The Wattenbergs weren't the kind of people to be sticking axes in their floors. They took better care of their house than that.''

''So you're saying what?'' Bret asked. ''That it was put here recently? Like maybe today? Or since we got here? I know we heard some noises, but we didn't hear an *ax*.''

''I know, I know,'' Erika said. ''It just seems . . . weird.''

''It *is* weird,'' Lynda said with a shiver. ''It's *gross*. But it's just wax.'' Her voice, however, did not sound convinced. In fact, she sounded as if she were trying desperately to convince herself not to scream at the top of her lungs.

With a slight smile Leslie said, ''There were always limbs scattered around this room. Remember when we used to come up here and just stare at them, as if we expected them to start moving or something. They were all so *real*-looking.''

''And the eyeballs,'' Bret said. ''Remember those? I always wanted one, but I could never work up the nerve to ask. I always wanted to take one home and scare the color out of my mother's face with it.''

They looked around the room for a while, browsed through the clothes on the rack, examined the few old tools and boxes of odds and ends on the dirty tables and shelves. But Erika could not take her attention entirely away from the pile of arms and legs beside the ax. Something about it gave her a sinking feeling; it looked too neat, too staged, as if someone had set it up for their benefit. She knew it sounded silly, but she wondered if perhaps the other girls were thinking the same thing. She noticed Leslie and Lynda glancing at the pile of wax limbs with suspicious eyes. Only Bret ignored them as if they weren't there, but then, that was something she would expect of Bret. Erika said nothing about it, though, just in case she was wrong and she was alone in her uneasiness.

When they left the workroom, Erika felt her muscles relax. If she'd looked behind her, she would have seen Lynda's and Leslie's shoulders sag a bit with relief, as well.

"Okay, you guys," Bret said on the way back downstairs. "Feel better now? Look, when we get back down there, I'll turn on some music so we won't hear all the squeaks and creaks in the house, okay?"

They reached the second floor and started down to the first, their flashlights illuminating the way before them. Bret was leading them, so she saw it first and slowed to a stop two-thirds of the way down the stairs.

"What's the matter?" Lynda asked.

Bret did not reply, so they tried to look beyond her.

The girls stared, and none of them moved or spoke for several long seconds.

Something was squatting in the dark at the bottom of the stairs.

Waiting.

Bret took a step down, then another, aiming her flashlight directly at the motionless figure. She released a breath explosively and let out a quiet, nervous laugh as she said, "It's only Little Miss Muffet sitting on her thing and eating her stuff."

The others started down behind Bret, silent.

"Whew," Bret sighed. "For a second there I thought it was some kind of—"

She froze. Her smile became a grimace.

The girls all looked at one another, mouths open.

Erika breathed the question they were all thinking: "How did it get here?"

Lynda put a hand over her mouth to muffle the whimper of fear that crawled up from her chest.

Erika murmured, "The noises . . . the pile of arms and legs and the ax upstairs . . . now this . . ."

"Somebody's here," Leslie whispered.

"Maybe some crazy person's been living here, and he's mad that we intruded," Erika said.

"That's impossible," Bret snapped, sounding a little angry. "How could anybody have gotten in? We had to break in!"

"Well, maybe someone came through the window after us," Leslie suggested. "Maybe . . . maybe one of those guys followed us . . . maybe *both* of them."

"That's possible," Erika whispered, looking around nervously in the dark.

"And this place is so big . . . who knows where they could be hiding. There may even be secret places we don't know about," Leslie said.

Lynda shook her head, as if she knew something they didn't, then said, "I want to go. Now. Right now. Okay?"

"I agree," Erika said. "Let's just get our things and leave. We can go out the front door; it'll be easier. We can just unlock it and get out of here."

Bret nodded. "Okay. Let's go."

They crossed the room under the agonizing gaze of the wax Christ and went into the Fantasy room. The beams cut unsteadily through the darkness because of the girls' trembling hands, and although the girls had been chattering happily only a few moments ago, the only sound now was their footsteps on the wood floor, and then even that sound died.

The girls stopped, flashlights aimed. They couldn't see the food and drinks spread over the two blankets because the blankets were surrounded.

Jack Horner sat facing them, but now, instead of a pie, he held a bag of potato chips on his lap.

Alice appeared to be reaching for a can of soda; the White Rabbit already held one between his furry paws.

Bilbo and Gandalf seemed to be deciding what they wanted as they stepped toward the food.

Humpty Dumpty sat on his wall, overlooking the gathering with his expression of panic.

Erika took a few steps forward as ice water flowed through her veins and chilled her entire body. She shined her flashlight between the hobbit and the wizard. The spider that had been suspended over Little Miss Muffet earlier was now on a six-pack of soda, guarding the drinks from the others.

It took her a moment, but Erika finally found her voice and croaked, "I-I don't think we should b-be here."

"Me, neither," Lynda said. She turned and pulled Leslie with her toward the door.

"Well, wait a second," Leslie said. "I need to get my coat."

"Get it later," Bret told her as they all started out of the room.

"That's a *cashmere coat*!" Leslie rasped.

"Front door," Erika said as they hurried into the Great Moments in History room.

"Do you know how much that coat cost?" Leslie squeaked.

"Get it later," Bret repeated.

The curtain hanging in the doorway that led to the front of the house was now thin and tattered and speckled with holes. Erika and Bret brushed it aside as they passed through with Lynda and Leslie behind them.

"We'll go straight to the police," Erika said.

"But we broke in here—won't we get into trouble?" Lynda asked.

"We're teenagers," Bret replied. "They *expect* that, it's what we *do*."

Cobwebs brushed their faces like the hair of passing ghosts, making them cringe as they hurried through the dark.

They reached the front door.

"Oh, no," Erika groaned in a voice so full of dread that it didn't sound like hers.

Something silver glimmered in the beams of light.

A hasp had been screwed to the two doors, locked by a fat, shiny padlock.

Erika lifted her flashlight and found another, identical lock just a couple feet above the first.

"What's going on here?" Bret whispered.

"These locks are new," Leslie said. "They're *obviously* brand new."

"Okay, okay, look," Erika said, "we don't know why these locks are here. Maybe whoever takes care of this place put them here."

"But why on the *inside*?" Bret asked. "That doesn't make sense."

Lynda whispered tremulously, "Please, let's

go. Let's just go out the way we came, okay? I don't like this; I don't like it at all."

"Okay," Bret said, "we'll go out the bathroom window." She turned and led them back through the curtained doorway, past the stairs and through the door that led into the Wattenbergs' old living quarters.

The girls moved faster now than they had before. Their lights bobbed through the darkness, the beams crossing again and again as they went through the living room, through the kitchen, and down the hall.

When they reached the bathroom door, Lynda let out an anguished yelp.

The other girls just stared in wide-eyed disbelief.

On the bathroom door was another hasp.

And another lock.

EIGHT

Trapped

A maniac, Erika thought. *We're in here with a maniac who wants us to stay in here.*

Bret was thinking so many things as she stared at the lock that she could scarcely single out one thought. She was feeling sorry—even guilty—for talking the girls into going inside the Waxhouse; she was frantically trying to latch onto an explanation and just as frantically trying to think of a way for them to get out of the house. Then a pale, bloated thought rose to the surface of her mind, a thought that nauseated her: Greg. She started to speak, but kept her mouth shut. For now.

It's a joke, Leslie thought over and over. *It's a joke, it has to be, it* has *to be a joke*. She finally said, "Okay, this is, like, a joke, right? I mean, one of you, like, set this all up, right?"

"We didn't set this up," Bret whispered. "It would have been *impossible* for one of us to set this up."

"It's not a joke," Lynda whispered, shaking her head slowly, still staring at the lock. "It's her."

"Who?" Erika asked.

"Karin."

There was a deadly silence as they stared, dumbfounded, at Lynda. Erika felt a cold sensation in the back of her throat.

"Oh, Lynda, Karin's *dead*," Bret said.

"But she's supposed to be here," Lynda went on. "We were all supposed to meet here today. And . . . and we were talking about her earlier . . ."

Erika went to Lynda's side and put a hand on her shoulder. "It's not Karin," she whispered. "You're just scared. We're all scared. We're just going to have to think of a way to get out of here." She realized she was talking to herself as much as to Lynda.

Erika and Bret exchanged a glance, and although they'd been connected only by letters and phone calls over the past six years, each of them knew from that glance that they were thinking the same thing; they were thinking about how bad this situation could get.

"The first thing we should do, I think," Bret

said, "is find a room we can lock from the inside and lock ourselves in."

"Good idea," Leslie said.

Erika whispered, "How about the bedroom?"

Without thinking about it twice, the girls turned and headed back down the hall until they came to the bedroom once occupied by Mr. and Mrs. Wattenberg. Inside they scanned the room with their lights to make sure they didn't have any company, then Erika closed the door.

"It doesn't lock," she said.

"*What?*" Lynda hissed.

"There's no lock," Erika repeated. "I guess there was no reason for one. They were the only ones living here."

"Give me your flashlight," Bret said to Erika. She looked around the room carefully. There was an old bed frame, two small nightstands, and a large dresser.

"How about this," Bret said, moving to the dresser. "We can put it in front of the door. Come give me a hand. It looks heavy."

The four of them gathered around the dresser, tucked flashlights beneath their arms, and hooked their fingers wherever they could get a good grip.

"Okay, let's drag it," Bret said.

The dresser groaned heavily over the wood floor as the girls pushed and pulled it away from the wall. There was a sudden rushing sound around their feet, a skittering that sent them staggering backward away from the dresser, gasping.

Something moved over Lynda's foot until she kicked her leg up and sent that something squeaking into the darkness.

Leslie felt something catch on her nylon and shimmy up her left leg beneath her skirt. When kicking her leg did no good, she dropped her flashlight and began swatting at her leg, making little sounds of fear and disgust.

Her flashlight clunked to the floor and rolled slowly, spilling its light over the girls' feet.

The girls saw them.

Mice.

They scattered in every direction out from beneath and behind the dresser and over the floor, some of them scurrying up a leg before dropping to the floor again and hurrying into the darkness.

Screams rang through the musty house as the girls dashed for the door of the bedroom. Bret hurried back to sweep up the dropped flashlight, then followed the others out and pulled the door shut behind her.

They stood in the hallway for a while, leaning against the walls and panting to catch their breath.

"Can anybody besides me hear my heart?" Erika gasped.

"Not over the sound of mine," Leslie said.

Between breaths Bret said, "I think . . . if I

cleared my throat right now . . . my heart would shoot out of my mouth.''

Only Lynda said nothing. She leaned back against the wall, shoulders rising and falling rapidly with each breath, staring up at the ceiling; her flashlight was pointed upward, and the light hit her face from below, giving her a ghostly look, making her face a white, deeply creased mask.

''Lynda?'' Erika said. ''You okay?''

''We shouldn't have come,'' she whispered. Her voice was thick and wet, as if she were holding back tears.

''I know.'' Bret sighed. ''And I'm sorry. My fault. We'll just have to find a way out and—''

''No, we won't find a way out,'' Lynda went on. ''She won't let us. She's been waiting for us to come, just as we agreed to six years ago.'' A tear finally made its way down her cheek, sparkling in the flashlight's harsh beam. ''She's been waiting for us because she knows . . . she knew all along . . . about the things we said about her . . . the things *I* said about her . . .''

''But you didn't say anything worse than we did,'' Erika told her, trying, but failing, to sound reassuring.

Lynda just shook her head slightly, closed her teary eyes, and whispered, ''Let's just go. Please. Let's go. Let's get out of here.''

''Yeah,'' Bret said, ''that's what we're going to do. I just don't know *how*.''

"There's a back door in the kitchen, isn't there?" Erika asked.

"I bet I know what we'll find," Leslie said.

"You're probably right," Bret replied, "but let's take a look, anyway."

Their feet crunched over the gritty floor as they went into the kitchen and looked around for the door. It was on the far side of the room. The window in the top half of the door—once decorated with cheerful yellow drapes—was now boarded up on the outside.

There was another shiny silver lock on the door.

After they'd stared silently at the lock for a moment, Bret said, "Okay, there's, um . . . well, there's just *got* to be an explanation for this."

No one commented.

"Maybe we can get out one of the windows," Leslie suggested.

"I don't know," Bret said. "Most of those boards looked pretty strong."

"We can try," Erika said. "But what if—"

There was a sound in the house, a muffled clump that made the girls jerk with surprise. There were several more clumps, as if someone very heavy were walking across the floor of another room.

The girls looked at one another with saucer-like eyes, but didn't move a fraction of an inch.

The noise continued for a bit, then stopped.

A moment later it began again, slow and deliberate, and then—

Silence.

When the girls finally moved, they closed the gaps between them until they were standing close, clinging to one another's arms.

"What are we going to do?" Leslie asked. Her voice vibrated with fear.

"Find a window with some loose boards nailed over it," Erika whispered. She could barely control her voice, as well. Her throat felt tight, as if a hand were clenching over it in a stranglehold. She glanced at Lynda. There was a look in the girl's eyes that worried Erika; it was something more than just fear, something approaching, perhaps, the edge of hysteria. Hoping to calm Lynda, if only a little, Erika took her hand.

"Why don't we start here?" Bret said, going to the two windows over the oval formica-and-chrome kitchen table. As Leslie pulled away one of the two chairs, Bret dragged the table away from the wall and stepped around it to the first window. It was locked, so she tried to pull the latch free. It wouldn't budge. The window had been painted shut. So had the other one. "Well." She sighed, picking up the chrome-framed chair. "It worked last time." She slammed the chair into the window and jumped backward quickly as the pane shattered and the chair bounced off the boards on the other side, then fell to the floor.

They stopped, listened, and waited for some reaction to the sound, some kind of response from somewhere deep in the house. They heard nothing.

Knocking pieces of glass out of her way with the toe of her shoe, Bret stepped forward again, stared for a moment at the boards that blocked the window, then, unexpectedly, slammed her shoulder into them. Again and again and again. Then she stopped and rubbed her shoulder as she said, "I don't like the feel of that."

"Sturdy?" Erika asked.

"*Real* sturdy. I think I need a chiropractor."

Bits of glass crunched under their feet as they moved toward Bret. They said nothing for a moment, just stood there, thoughtful and silent —except for Lynda, who looked more nervous than thoughtful, glancing around now and then as if she expected something awful to happen at any moment.

"You think there might be some tools upstairs? In the workroom?" Leslie asked. "Something we might use to break through the boards?"

"That's a good idea," Erika said. "I think we should check it out."

"I don't want to go back up there," Lynda breathed. "Please, let's just find another way out."

"There *is* no other way out," Erika replied. "We have to *make* a way out, and to do that, we'll need tools. So we *have* to go upstairs to find some.''

''We'll stick together, Lynda,'' Leslie reassured her, ''and we'll be fine.''

But they were all just as frightened as Lynda looked. None of them could deny that they were not alone in the big house.

Erika, for one, felt somehow safer in the Wattenbergs' living quarters. In spite of the musty darkness and the fact that the house had been abandoned, these rooms felt, in an odd way, warmer, more comforting, and she was reluctant to leave them and go into the wax museum.

Bret, on the other hand, did not feel safe *anywhere* in the old house. But she did not let any hint of her fear show itself to her friends.

They left the kitchen, went through the living room, and slowed to a stop when they came to the curtained doorway that would take them into the Waxhouse.

The curtain shifted slightly, back and forth. A draft caused by their movements or—

Something else?

Erika looked at Bret, who shrugged with resignation. The two of them pushed through the doorway first.

There was nothing on the other side but darkness.

They moved through Great Moments in History, paused for just a moment at the foot of the stairs, then started up.

Flashlight beams bobbed up the steps, bouncing from side to side. One beam—it was from Erika's light—slid up the steps smoothly, all the way up until it stopped at the top of the staircase and Erika screamed.

The light landed on a white, bulbous face with two round, nonhuman eyes and a grotesque mouth, open as if to bite, and—the creature lurched forward, rushing down the stairs toward the girls.

NINE

Unfriendly Darkness

The girls began to scramble away frantically, stumbling down the stairs as the creature tumbled toward them, a blur of eyes and mouth and puffy white hands.

Screams shot through the darkness and flashlights hit the steps and rolled as first Lynda and then Bret fell backward, clamoring down the stairs with grunts and cries of pain. They nearly pulled Erika and Leslie down with them before tumbling off the stairs and across the floor, with the other two girls hurrying off the steps right behind them.

Their pursuer landed next with a solid thud, then rolled over the wood floor with a low rumble.

There was a clackety-clack sound on the

stairs as a black, sticklike arm with a puffy, white-gloved hand followed its owner.

Erika regained her balance, heart thundering and lungs gasping for breath as adrenaline electrified her whole body. Leslie stood beside her, hands shaking as if afflicted with palsy, clutching Erika's arm. Bret and Lynda both crawled crablike on their backs away from the stairs and the thing that had come down after them.

Thunderous silence, except for their raspy breaths.

Then Leslie began to tremble with laughter as she stared at the thing on the floor.

Aiming her flashlight at it, Erika said hoarsely, "Humpty Dumpty had a great fall."

The giant egg lolled back and forth, its startled face gazing up at them as if to ask for help. Its remaining arm was broken between the elbow and the three-fingered hand, and it dangled at a gruesome angle. As it rocked to one side, its left eyeball plopped out and fell to the floor. Erika's flashlight tracked the eyeball as it rolled slowly away from Humpty Dumpty, bumping to a halt against Lynda's shoe. The eye glared up at her coldly where she lay, the light shining on its glossy, wet-looking surface.

With a sudden burst of breath and a strangled sound of disgust, Lynda kicked the eyeball away. It rattled into the darkness and bounced off walls, finally falling silent.

"I want to get out of here," she whispered. "I want to get out of here *right now*."

"We *all* do, Lynda," Bret said as she got to her feet. "And we're *going* to get out of here. But if you don't stop *saying* that, I'm going to have to slap you in the face, just the way they do in the movies, so knock it off. Now . . . is anybody hurt?" she asked, looking around.

After a moment the other girls shook their heads.

"Okay, good," Erika said, looking up the stairs. She saw nothing, but knew that didn't mean nothing was there. "Are we still going up to the workroom?" she asked.

"That's probably the only place we'll find any tools," Bret replied, retrieving her flashlight. She started up the stairs, shining it before her, holding it in a tense hand almost as if it were a weapon. When she heard nothing behind her, she stopped, turned to them, and said, "Well?"

Erika led the others up the stairs behind Bret, who slowed her pace as she neared the top, moving the flashlight back and forth cautiously.

They started up the next flight without incident. At the top they hurried into the attic and closed the door behind them. They paused a moment as the silence in the large room gave way to a whisper that grew louder in a rush, until the attic echoed with the sound of heavy rainfall.

"Okay," Erika said, "start looking for anything that might get us out of here."

Leslie added, "Might be a good idea to look for weapons, too."

They moved around the tables and cabinets in the room, slowly so they wouldn't miss anything. All the surfaces were coated with grimy dust, and cobwebs filled the corners of cupboards and shelves. Insects chittered across tabletops, disturbed by the girls' search.

In the drawers and on the shelves, there were a number of tools left behind by their owners, tools now black and stiff from neglect and the unfriendly darkness in which they had been abandoned; odd-shaped tools, some of which looked as if they'd come from the set of an old mad scientist movie. When they were children, the girls had thought the tools looked exotic and mysterious; fascinated, they'd watched the Wattenbergs use them with surprising dexterity, in spite of their knobby hands.

Now the tools simply looked useless.

"I can't find anything," Bret mumbled, unable to keep the tension from her voice. She saw that her hands were shaking, and she hated it, tried to ignore it.

Tools clanked together. Drawers rattled open and shut. Feet clumped on the floor.

"I can't find *anything*," Bret said again, louder and more forcefully this time.

"What about this?" Leslie asked.

106

Erika and Bret hurried to her side and looked at the object she held. It was a slim, two-foot-long iron bar with one end that narrowed to a chisellike edge.

"What is that?" Bret asked. "What's it for?"

Erika replied, "Who cares, if it'll get us out of here."

"Well, we can give it a try," Leslie said. "It's better than nothing."

"It won't work," Lynda whispered. Her voice came from behind them, and the three girls turned to see Lynda standing at a vent, staring out through the slats, her back to them.

"We can try," Erika said.

She shook her head slowly, staring outside into the rain as she gradually lowered herself to her knees and curled her fingers around the edge of one of the slats.

"It won't do any good," she whispered. "We aren't going to get out of here because she doesn't want us to."

The girls turned slowly to one another; their eyes said, *Uh-oh*.

"Lynda?" Erika said hesitantly. "We're not sure *who's* in the house with us, but we *are* going to get out so we can—"

"It's *her*, can't you *feel* it?" Lynda let go of the slat on the vent and turned to them, pressing her back to the wall and hugging herself. "And don't tell me again she's *dead*; I *know* she's dead. That's why all this is happening. Do you really think that if some crazy man,

107

some psycho, was in a big house with four helpless teenage girls, he'd play tricks? No! He'd have his way with us, then slit our throats . . . or . . . or tie us up and throw us in a van and take us across the country and sell us to pornographers, or something, but it wouldn't be like this. No, this is different. It's her, I'm *telling* you, it's *her*. She's come to meet with us on the day we agreed to meet. And . . . she's come because of me . . . because of what I . . . what I said to her once . . . what I never apologized for, even though I knew, later, that it must've hurt her . . . hurt her terribly, because . . . I was supposed to be her friend. She's come because of how I must have made her feel. Believe me . . . we're not getting out of here, because Karin doesn't *want* us to . . .''

TEN

Revelations

A few minutes later the girls were sitting in a haphazard circle, listening cautiously for more sounds of movement in the house. They had found three dusty chairs stacked in a corner of the attic, and Bret sat on a wooden crate.

Erika was shocked to find that her hands were trembling. She'd been shaken by what Lynda had said. What had Lynda been talking about? What had she said to Karin that could have been so hurtful?

Could it have been the same kind of thing Erika had said to her? Something that was said with the best of intentions, but that was, she realized later, really cruel coming from a friend—especially from one of the only friends Karin had?

"Okay, listen," Erika said, leaning forward and putting her elbows on her knees. "We're all upset about Karin's death, Lynda, but I think maybe . . . well, maybe you're carrying it a little bit too far."

Lynda gave her a half smile. "You mean, maybe I'm, like, hysterical?"

Erika said, "Well, I didn't exactly say you were—"

"Uh-uh. I'm *not* hysterical." The half smile fell away as quickly as it had come and was replaced by a lost, sad look, as if she were about to cry but could not quite pinpoint the reason. "I did something wrong to Karin," she whispered.

"We were *all* making fun of her that night," Bret said. "It wasn't just you, so don't—"

"No, I'm not talking about that night. It was before that. Not long after she started hanging around with us. It was at my house. I . . . I invited her over for dinner. After we ate, I took her to my room. We were thumbing through books and magazines and stuff, and all of a sudden, like out of the blue, she asks, 'Lynda, why don't the other kids at school like me?' " She stopped, closed her eyes, and took a deep breath. "I didn't know what to say. I mean, what *could* I say. So I figured I'd be honest and try to—" She laughed then, an icy, bitter laugh. "Try to help her out. So I said . . . I said, 'Well, you know, Karin, it might help if you lost a little weight. Maybe went on a diet, or something. You know, lots of fruits and vegetables, and no junk food?' She just stared at me. A flat, *nothing* stare. So I said, 'Well, it couldn't *hurt*, you know. And maybe you could do something with your hair? I mean, so it's not just sitting there, stringy, like it is. You know, curl it, put it up, maybe have it styled, something.' And still . . . she just stared at me like that, as if she were somewhere else, or something. It was kind of spooky, you know? So I stopped. I didn't say anymore. But I think I said enough. I thought about it a lot later, about how she must have felt. At the time I thought I was saying the right thing. But later . . . I didn't think so. Now I *know* it was the wrong thing. We were the only friends she had. *Period*. And I said those things to her. I pretty much told her she was fat and ugly. Might as *well* have told her that. I hurt her. I hurt her bad. And now she's come to . . . to hurt me back.''

Erika stared at Lynda for a long moment, but her vision was blurred; she was lost in thought, thinking of what *she* had said to Karin one day years ago, and suddenly Lynda's claim that Karin had come to meet with them did not seem so impossible. She jerked her head back and forth to rid her mind of such ridiculous notions and looked around at the others. She

111

felt no better, though, because their faces reflected her thoughts.

The girls, all looking very troubled, stared at Lynda. Bret chewed a thumbnail. Leslie bowed her head slowly. No one spoke. No one appeared to *want* to speak; each of them seemed too preoccupied with her own thoughts.

"I did the same thing," Leslie finally whispered. Her brow was furrowed, and she turned her eyes from Lynda to stare into the dark. "I felt bad about it, too. For a long time. I still do. And it's funny because . . . well, because it was almost the exact same conversation. She asked me why the other kids didn't like her, why they made fun of her, and I told her it might help if . . . if she fixed herself up a little. I told her what clothes would be best for her, because . . . well, come *on*, she didn't exactly dress for . . . you know, for her *figure*. Anyway . . . I told her pretty much the same things as Lynda. About her hair, her, um, weight. That sort of thing."

Bret's troubled look had been replaced by a frown. Her mouth hung open, and she squinted at Leslie.

"Wait, hold it, just wait a second," Bret said, holding up her hands. "You're telling me Karin's ghost has come back to haunt us because we told her . . . well, we told her . . . okay, I said the same kinds of things to her once, all right? She asked me the very same question once in the Burger Barrel, and I told her she should clean up her act. I mean, lose weight, dress better, fix her hair, all of that. But what's the big deal? I mean, it was all the *truth*, right?''

''Not exactly,'' Erika said. Her voice was dry and cracked when she spoke. ''None of us gave her the right answer to her question.''

The others turned to her and stared, their faces white as flour.

''I did it, too,'' Erika said. ''It's bugged me ever since, and I'm ashamed to admit it now, but I answered the same question the same way.''

''Well, what were we supposed to say?'' Bret asked. She didn't sound bitter or malicious, just genuinely curious.

''We were her only friends, Bret,'' Erika said. ''Her *only* friends. She respected our opinions and took what we said seriously, and we did not give her the right answer. Do you really think the other kids at school didn't like her because she was fat and unattractive and didn't dress as nicely as the others and always had stringy hair?''

The other three girls exchanged cautious glances, and Bret finally shrugged and said, ''Well . . . yes, I think that's about right.''

''Well, if so, then we shouldn't have said there was anything wrong with her, we should have told her there was something wrong with *them*, because those are all the *wrong* reasons not to like someone you don't even *know*, right?'' When she got no response, she went on: "I've always figured I must have really hurt her, but now that I know you guys told her the same thing . . . well, we *really* must have hurt her. I mean . . . we told her that she was unlikable, really, right? We told her she was too fat and too ugly for anyone to like her, right? Can you *imagine* how she felt? Hearing that from the only friends she had in the world? No *wonder* she said those things the last time we saw her here."

Leslie stood and walked slowly to the vent. One of the slats had been bent outward and upward, so she could look out instead of just down. She was able to see the market across the street. The lights out front glowed in the misty darkness of the early night. Then she saw something that took her mind off Karin for a moment.

"Hey, you guys," she whispered, "come here and take a look at this."

They all went to the vent and peered between the slats at the froglike man hunched forward in his wheelchair, alone in front of the store, parked beneath a short awning that protected him from the drizzle. His hands hung over his lap between the armrests, twitching and jittering restlessly. The light was not good, but he appeared to be staring at the Waxhouse; his head rocked back and forth now and then as he laughed at something that only he found amusing.

"Do you . . ." Leslie's dry voice cracked, and

she stopped to swallow. "Do you think he's laughing at us?"

Before any of them could reply, there was a sound from just outside the attic door, the sound of something thumping down on the wood floor and then—a laugh, a high, shrieking laugh.

Lynda began to cry quietly. Leslie, far behind her, managed to hold back her tears for a while. Bret simply stared at the closed door with her mouth hanging open and her eyebrows raised high; after a moment her chest began to rise and fall rapidly as her breaths came faster. Erika felt tears burn her eyes as she turned to the door and stared, listening.

"This is crazy," Bret whispered. "This is . . . I mean, really, this is . . . *insane*."

"You *heard* it," Lynda croaked through her tears. "You heard it your*self*!"

Bret put down her flashlight, stood slowly, and took the short iron bar from Leslie, shaking her head slightly from side to side as she moved cautiously away from the girls and toward the door. She stood before it for a long time. The other girls sat rigid in their chairs, watching.

A wind had come up outside and was growing stronger. It blew rain against the house hard and made the walls creak against its pressure.

Bret put one hand on the doorknob and lifted the bar, ready to use it if necessary.

"Bret," Erika whispered, fear quivering in her voice, "maybe you shouldn't—"

Bret pulled the door open in one sudden movement and let out a long, garbled scream as a tall, dark figure dived through the doorway and, arms outstretched, threw itself on her.

ELEVEN

Desperation

Their screams reverberated in the attic as Bret used the iron bar to repeatedly bludgeon the skull of her attacker. She struggled beneath his weight, kicking and squirming, until the body crumbled off of her in pieces that clattered over the floor, stiff and lifeless.

Bret hardly noticed; she rolled away and bounded to her feet, dashing across the room to where the other girls now stood gawking. Bret was spitting a stream of breathless profanity so quickly that all the words seemed to blend together into one long amalgamated obscenity. She skidded to a halt and spun around, her fist still clutching the bar, her arm still poised to strike. Her arm lowered slowly as she squinted at the body lying in a heap in a pool of light.

"Dracula," Erika said, surprised that she could even speak through her fear.

The disassembled figure wore a black cape with red lining. The body had broken at the waist, and the head—pale skin, black hair with a widow's peak, slightly pointed ears, and, of course, two sharp white fangs—had snapped off and rolled a couple feet away. The outstretched arms, pale fingers curled to clutch a victim, had broken off and lay on each side of the body.

"Another one," Leslie rasped.

"Just a dummy," Bret said, still out of breath. "Just another damned dummy." She picked up her flashlight and tossed a glance at Erika. The two of them went over to the wax dummy on the floor, closely followed by Leslie and Lynda.

"She put it there," Lynda said, still sniffling. "*She* leaned that thing against the door. She's doing this, she's *playing* with us. *You* heard her laugh outside the door, right? She's trying to *scare* us. I thought it was just me, that *I* was the only one who'd said such a thing to her, but now I know it's *all* of us—and that's why she's come." She was talking faster now, her voice reaching a breathless fever pitch. "It's like she's . . . she's . . . she's, I don't know, like she's getting *back* at us. For telling her those things, for telling her she wasn't *good* enough,

118

that she was too fat, too-too . . . she's getting back at us for . . . for hurting her . . . for being her only friends in the world and hurting her and . . . I'm scared." She hugged herself with unsteady arms. "I mean, what are we going to—how are we going to—oh, my god, I'm so scared."

Erika turned to find Bret staring at her, as if silently asking for help, and Erika took her hand and squeezed it. Fear looked out of place in Bret's eyes.

Could Lynda be right? It was ridiculous, silly, completely unbelievable, but . . . could she be right?

"I don't know," Leslie whispered, her mouth dry. "This sounds crazy, I mean, really crazy, but . . . maybe not *too* crazy, know what I mean?"

Erika felt the skin on the back of her neck shrivel, and goose bumps crawled over her scalp.

Suddenly Bret dropped the bar, bounded over the wax dummy and out the attic door onto the stairs. They heard her take in a deep breath, then she shouted—no, *screamed*—"Is that you, Greg? Are you doing this crap? Because if you are, you can stop it! You've made your stupid *point*, okay? You hear me? I promise I won't go out with any other guys, and I'll return all your calls and make time for you when you want to go out, and I won't talk about breaking up anymore if you'll just *knock it the hell off right now*!'' Her last word crumbled into a sob, and she backed through the doorway into the attic, leaning forward and covering her face with her hands as she cried softly.

Erika put an arm around her and whispered, ''Do you really think it's Greg?''

''I don't know,'' she said with a sniff, wiping her eyes. The crying had stopped quickly. ''Might be, might not be. I . . . don't know.'' She scrubbed her face, bent down to pick up the bar, took a deep breath, and sighed. ''Okay, what do we do now?''

They thought about that a moment, each of them nervously twitching in some way: Erika jittered her leg, Bret slapped her thigh with the bar, Leslie twirled a finger through her hair, and Lynda jerked her arms as she hugged herself with them.

''Let's try this first, okay?'' Erika asked, nodding toward the bar in Bret's hand.

''What if it doesn't work?'' Bret mumbled.

''We'll deal with that when it happens,'' Erika said.

''Just a sec,'' Leslie said, going to the vent again. After a moment she said, ''He's still there. Still . . . laughing, I think. Just laughing and looking over here.''

''Just as long as he stays over *there*,'' Bret said.

Leslie turned to them. ''Yeah, but what about his sons? Where are they?''

They were all silent for a long while, then Erika said, "Well, let's get moving."

Lynda nodded toward the stairs. "So . . . we have to . . . go down there . . . right?"

"Well." Bret laughed coldly. "I'm not jumping three stories."

Erika tried to calm herself before speaking again, but her voice was still unsteady. "Okay, so let's just stick close together and try not to panic."

They stepped over the wax body on their way out the door, all of them cringing a little, as if it were a real human corpse.

They headed downstairs, clumsily at first because they were all staying so close together. When they finally spread out—but only a bit, only enough to allow them to walk without falling—they moved more smoothly, although not very quickly. The beams of their flashlights flickered nervously through the darkness, as if the light itself were afraid of the dark, and when they reached the second-floor landing, they paused to look all around them, squinting to see as deep into the darkness as possible before continuing to the first floor.

Outside, the night had become angry. The wind slammed against the house and whipped around the corners with a faint, mournful wail.

They were a quarter of the way down the stairs when one of the flashlight beams fell on a face looking up at them from the steps.

Leslie screamed, stumbling backward and pulling Lynda with her.

The face belonged to a dirty-looking bearded man who was crawling naked up the stairs toward them, his eyes and mouth open wide, his arms out at his sides, his blood-streaked face turned up toward them.

The screams were brief. The girls stared down at the body, relieved, but still nervous.

It was the wax figure of Christ lying on the stairs, its eyes directed up at them. Even though they now knew otherwise, the wax figure still looked all too real and frightening. They walked the rest of the way down the stairs very slowly, careful not to touch the figure as they stepped over it.

None of them spoke as they headed for the kitchen and the window that Bret had broken earlier. They could hear one another's breathing, and each girl's ears pounded with a frantic heartbeat and the throbbing rush of adrenaline.

In the kitchen they stopped and faced the window.

"Okay," Bret said, handing her flashlight to Lynda and nodding to Erika. "Come give me some light for this."

Broken glass crunched beneath their feet as they went to the window. The wind continued to blow violently outside, and rain smacked against the boards nailed over the window, but no matter how hard the wind blew, no draft came inside between the boards. They had been nailed up securely, tightly.

Erika shined her light on the boards, and Bret tried to wedge the chisel end of the bar between two of them. Her movements were careful at first, precise, but when she was unsuccessful, she pushed a little harder, pumping the bar up and down as she tried to pry the end between two of the boards.

"It's like a wall!" she barked, trying again. And again and again.

She swung the bar backward like a baseball bat so suddenly that the others jumped away, startled; then she began to beat the boards, grumbling to herself in a low, gravelly voice. The sound made the other girls flinch and move back even farther, including Erika, who left Bret to pound the boards in the darkness.

"Stop it," Erika said, then shouted, *"Stop!"*

Bret spun around, panting and angry. "The end of this thing is too fat," she snapped, "and the boards are too tight. I swear, those things were nailed up by a carpenter." Her voice trembled, but behind the trembling, she sounded frustrated and angry.

Erika sighed and, trying to sound encouraging, said, "Well, then, I guess we try something else, right?"

"Like what?" Leslie asked.

Bret ran a hand through her hair and said hoarsely, "Well, I guess we're open for suggestions.'' She looked around at the others, but no one had any ideas.

The girls were too busy listening and watching.

Erika's eyes held on the bar in Bret's hand. ''Do you think you could break one of those padlocks with that?'' she asked.

Bret looked down at the bar. ''I don't know. Those things are pretty sturdy. Somebody did a good job of picking out the heaviest locks he could find. I just wish there were another window we could . . .'' She stopped. Her eyes widened slightly. ''Hey. On the way in here, did anybody notice boards over the basement window?''

''Basement window?'' Lynda asked, her voice still thick with tears.

''Yes. Remember the basement window? Not very big, but probably big enough for one of us. Mr. Wattenberg said he was going to cover it to keep the light out of the Chamber of Horrors—don't you remember? They were going to turn the back part of the basement into a torture chamber, he said. Remember?''

Finally their heads began to nod, one at a time, as the memory came back to them.

''Yeah,'' Leslie said, ''you're right. It was kind of like one of those . . . what do you call those old-fashioned windows they used to put above doors?''

''Transom windows?'' Erika asked.

"Yes, it was like one of those. But he covered it over, remember?"

A little more enthusiastic now, Bret said, "But only with some kind of thin black paneling. Something flimsy." She hefted the bar in her hand. "Something I might be able to break through with this."

"But do you want to go *down* there?" Lynda hissed.

"Look. I got you guys into this, right? I mean, it was my idea. I'm the one who practically dragged all of you in here against your will. So . . . it's only fair that I be the one to go down there and try to get through that window."

"And what if you get through?" Erika asked. "What will you do then?"

"Well . . . it's up to you. I can either call you down so you can go through with me, or I can walk around the house and try to get those boards off the kitchen window so you guys can climb out that way."

Without waiting for any kind of response, Bret spun away from them and left the kitchen. They hurried down the hall after her, stopping in front of the door with a sign over it that read:

CHAMBER OF HORRORS
Enter at your own risk

"I only ask one thing," Bret said. "That all of you stay right here, right outside this door.

Because if I come back up here and you're gone, I'm going to freak, and be a vegetable for the rest of my natural life, okay?''

''Are you sure you want to go down there by yourself?'' Leslie asked.

''You guys want to come with me?'' Bret asked.

Three heads shook negatively without hesitation.

''Okay.'' She turned around, tucked her flashlight under her arm, and opened the door. ''Wish me luck,'' she muttered as she descended into the tar black darkness.

The door slowly swung closed behind her.

It was as if the basement had swallowed her whole.

TWELVE

In the Chamber of Horrors

As she cautiously descended the creaky stairs, Bret could actually feel the darkness touching her, cold and moist and sly. It was so dense that even the flashlight beam seemed to shrink back away from it a bit, intimidated.

She thought back to the last time—the *only* time—she'd been down in the Chamber of Horrors, and that didn't make this visit any easier. Yes, she'd been just a kid then, a kid who was easily frightened and believed in monsters and ghosts. But now . . . well, now she was a *teenager* who was easily frightened and believed in monsters and ghosts.

She shined the flashlight downward, but still

did not see the bottom of the stairs. They seemed to go on forever.

Finally the light fell on the dirty floor below, and then it hit something else: the toe of a dusty black shoe sticking out from around the corner of the wall. The shoe did not move, just waited.

Bret raised the light slowly, very slowly, following a black pant leg up to a red vest over a white shirt. She gasped quietly when the light illuminated a familiar, but still frightening face: the Phantom of the Opera, face long and pale, head balding, teeth mangled and rotting. His bony right hand held his mask above his head, as if he'd just torn it from his face.

When she stepped off the bottom step, Bret heard small sounds of quick movement over the floor, skittering sounds that made her cringe.

As she moved around the room, she found that the chamber had been changed since her last visit. Black curtains had been put up to form a narrow passageway that twisted and turned, mazelike, through the darkness, occasionally opening up into a horrific scene starring motionless figures that appeared ready to move at any moment.

The first scene was a stone-walled laboratory in which Frankenstein's monster was bursting from his bonds as the mad doctor looked on in horror.

The next was a murky dungeon in which a

helpless woman raised her arms against some invisible horror. Bret shined the light around until she spotted a small sign that read, COUNT DRACULA. But the count, of course, had been relocated . . . and subsequently dismembered.

She moved on, past the Creature from the Black Lagoon, the Wolfman, and a mummy rising from its sarcophagus.

Then she came to a narrow curtained doorway below a large sign that read, HISTORICAL HORRORS. The sign was wrapped in a cocoon of cobwebs—real ones, not the fake stuff—and spiders crawled all over it.

Bret started to push the cobwebby curtain aside so she could go through, but froze for a moment when she heard more scurrying sounds on the floor. Those mice . . . She closed her eyes and imagined them . . . small, squirmy bodies wrapped in a coat of mangy fur the same color as the bottom of a garbage disposal . . . glistening, pinhead-size eyes . . . tiny, twitching mouths filled with even tinier, sharp-pointed teeth . . .

Bret sent up a little prayer that she wouldn't come across any more that night. Then she pushed through the curtain and entered a dungeon.

Great sheets of cobwebs hung from the corners above her; she couldn't tell which ones were real and which weren't.

The room was decorated with instruments of torture and execution from the past.

Two skeletons with bits of old clothes and some tattered flesh still clinging to their bones were chained to the stone wall, which was really just a plaster wall with a very deceptive, well-done paint job, no doubt courtesy of Mrs. Wattenberg.

Below the skeletons stood a figure wearing a black robe, the face lost in the dark shadow of the robe's hood; one arm was raised, fist clutching a knife with a long blade. The knife hovered over a young woman wearing rags and tied to a table.

A man was being stretched taut on the racks, his mouth open in a silent scream of pain as his hands and feet were pulled in opposite directions by a mean-looking, muscular thug who gleefully turned the crank on the large wooden contraption.

An iron maiden stood open, its deadly spikes reddened by blood, and inside stood a man, bloodied and full of holes, his face a death mask of shock and pain, his body limp and about to fall forward out of the upright casket.

A man tied faceup to a table, clothed only in a dirty loincloth, stared in horror at the round split-level cage resting on his abdomen. In the top half of the cage were lumps of hot, ruby red coal; just below the hot coals, in the bottomless half of the cage, were two large rats. Desperate to escape the heat, the rats had begun to chew through the man's skin, to burrow into his stomach.

Bret's lips slid back over her teeth, and she made a sound of disgust as she shuddered. She swept the light to her right and saw a guillotine. The blade had fallen; a head lay in a basket in front of it, a headless body on the floor behind it.

Next to that a limp body hung from a noose on a gallows. The neck was obviously broken, and Bret half expected the body to turn slowly on the rope, or perhaps twitch and jerk in its final seconds of movement.

More chittering movement on the floor. She darted the light back and forth but saw nothing. She shined it on the wall and tried to find the place where the window should be.

Where the stone paint job ended, the wall was black in the corner and covered mostly with cobwebs. If she remembered correctly, the window was somewhere behind that black paneling, just below the ceiling. If she could pull—or break—the paneling away from the top down, she knew she'd find it. But she'd need something to stand on.

She went to the table that held the man being eaten by rats. Close up, he looked dusty, but no less realistic or disgusting. She wondered how a couple of sweet old folks like the Wattenbergs could create something so horrible. It seemed as if she should be able to hear the wet chewing noises of the rats eating their way into the prisoner's abdomen. He was chained to the table, arms and legs spread in four directions, so she wouldn't be able to simply knock him to the floor and out of her way. Bret stared at the wax figure for a moment, deciding she would have to force the poor, tortured fellow out of his shackles. She lifted the bar, chisel end down, and brought it down hard, stabbing it into the figure's right wrist. The hand broke off with a dull, ugly crack, and the figure jerked, as if reacting in pain.

Bret did the same with the other wrist and both ankles, then slid the body off the table. It smacked to the floor, and the cage that had covered the two rats rolled away on its side into the dark.

Hands and feet remained in the iron bonds, and the chains rattled around as Bret pushed the table over to the corner of the room. The heavy legs scraped over the concrete floor with a shrill grating sound. Bret leaned on the table and was about to climb up onto it when—she heard a sound, a very familiar sound, beneath the table.

Clickety-chick-chicket-clickety-clickety.

She felt something on her feet. She shrieked, throwing herself on the table, and began kicking her legs frantically, hoping to rid them of any hangers-on.

On hands and knees Bret looked over the edge of the table and saw tiny vague shapes skittering around the floor in the darkness. She shined the flashlight down there and caught one of the little creature's in the beam. The mouse froze and stared up at her, its whiskers fidgeting on each side of its pointy face, then it was gone, as quickly as if it had evaporated into the dank air.

"Yecchhh," Bret spat, shuddering.

She picked up the bar and stood, facing the wall. Her hair brushed against the ceiling. She lifted the bar and pounded the wall with it.

The surface was solid. No window.

She tried again. And again and again.

There was another noise behind and below her, and she spun around and aimed the flashlight at the floor.

No mice.

But something was there.

She stared at the room for a long time, moving the flashlight back and forth slowly.

Yes, something about the room was different, she had no doubt. She just couldn't figure out what it was. Something had changed, and yet it hadn't changed enough for her to single it out.

Bret stared a moment longer, then went back to pounding the wall. Finally the bar cracked the paneling with a loud splintering sound.

"Ah-hah!" she blurted, smiling. "Gotcha." She pounded at the crack enthusiastically until the bar broke through the paneling. Prying the bar back and forth, Bret allowed herself a little laugh of satisfaction as the pressed board crunched like breaking bone. It was stubborn, though, and she had to fight it to make any progress. She stopped for a moment and took a deep breath, then leaned forward to start again.

Suddenly the sound came again. This time it *didn't* sound like mice.

Bret turned slowly and passed the light over the room again, frowning. The sound had resembled that of feet moving over the concrete behind her.

"Huh-hello?" she asked, her voice dry and crackly. "Any . . . body there? Erika? Leslie? Lynda? Are you guys—"

Bret's words caught in her throat when she noticed something . . . or *thought* she noticed something. The wax figure in the black hooded robe seemed to be standing in a different place than it had been when Bret had come in.

But she wasn't sure.

The figure had been standing over the woman tied to the table, knife raised high above its head, ready to drive it into the helpless victim. At least, that was how it had looked to Bret. Now the figure seemed farther away from the table and closer to Bret.

In fact . . . it *was* . . . wasn't it? The knife did not seem to be over the table any longer. It seemed—

Two mice darted across the floor, zigzagging.

"It's *you*," Bret hissed. "*You're* making me jumpy, you little twits."

134

Ignoring the trembling in her arms and hands, she turned around and began prying the paneling away from the window again. The flashlight beam reflected on the windowpane, and Bret felt her heartbeat quicken with excitement rather than fear. Not only had she found the window, but she could not see any boards blocking it on the other side.

"I was right," she whispered to herself. "I *knew* I was right. Well, I *thought* I was right . . . but I *was* right." She giggled at the frantic sound of her own voice as she began to pry more of the paneling away. It was difficult with only one hand, however, so she tucked the flashlight under her arm and held the bar in both hands, grunting as she pushed and pulled as hard as she could. She didn't want to waste any time in clearing the way to the window so they could all—

There was a sudden rush of movement behind her, faster and more distinct than before, and so startling that she spun around quickly and clumsily enough to drop both the bar and the flashlight.

The bar clunked on the tabletop, then clanged to the floor.

The flashlight stayed on the table, but rolled this way and that at Bret's feet, wobbling its light dizzyingly through the darkness.

Bret stood frozen in place, staring into the darkness. She held her breath without realizing it, her eyes searching, trying to follow the light that rolled back and forth, back and forth.

Bret gasped.

The black-robed figure was gone.

Her mouth opened, but nothing came out. She looked down at the bar on the floor a few feet from the table. It was her only weapon—the flashlight was the long, heavy kind, but wouldn't do nearly as much damage—but she couldn't seem to make herself move to retrieve it.

In a hoarse whisper she said, "Greg? Is that you? Please . . . please stop this. Please—" She coughed, and her voice became more solid, but was still very unsteady. "Greg? I promise I'll . . . I'll be the way you want me to be if . . . if you'll just stop this, because . . . because you're scaring me!"

She watched and waited.

There was no movement, no sound except the inner explosions of her heart. Finally Bret made herself bend over and pick up the flashlight. Then she carefully got off the table and leaned over for the bar.

A mouse skittered over it with a tiny squeak.

Bret let out a yelp and jerked her outreached hand to her chest as she stood up suddenly and stumbled backward. She bumped into something, which frightened her even more, and with an even louder cry, she spun around and—her voice became a strangled gurgle, then fell silent.

Bret stood scant inches from the black-robed figure. The face was still invisible in the hood. The arm remained frozen in the air, knife pointing downward. Unlike everything else down here, the blade had no blood on it. It was clean and shiny and reflected the light in a quick silver flash.

She couldn't breathe, couldn't blink, couldn't even move her mouth. Her arm moved, almost of its own accord, and lifted the flashlight slowly. The beam slid up the motionless figure, flowed over the robe's folds and wrinkles as it worked its way up, and finally stopped on the face that was all but swallowed inside the sacklike hood, framed by the blood red lining.

The face . . .

Bret was certain her heart would stop at any moment.

Her skin seemed to tighten until she felt certain it would split open and spill its contents onto the concrete.

She felt as lifeless and stiff as the wax figures around her as she stared at the familiar face, until she managed, somehow, to breathe a few words:

"No, no, no . . . please . . . *don't—*"

The face smiled a cruel, hateful smile.

Bret suddenly sucked in a breath to scream to the girls upstairs, to warn them, to call them, but she was able to get only an abrupt sound out, no more than a fraction of the scream she'd intended.

The knife swept down in an instant.

The blade's silver flash sliced into Bret.

She never felt the floor as it ended her fall.

THIRTEEN

Fear and Suspicion

"I heard something," Lynda hissed, spinning around to face the door behind them.

"I think I did, too," Erika whispered.

Leslie asked, "What? What was it?"

"Well, it sounded like Bret, but . . . I'm not sure," Erika replied.

So they stood there, silent and listening.

Wind and rain still attacked the house from outside, and inside it was growing cold enough so the girls could see a hint of vapor in front of their faces whenever they exhaled. The house was alive with noises—creaks and shifts and moaning sounds—all from the raucous weather . . . at least, so the girls hoped.

But this new sound was different. It had definitely come from beyond the basement door.

But the sound did not occur again.

"What should we do?" Leslie asked.

Erika didn't answer for a while. Even if it hadn't been Bret, Erika figured it couldn't hurt to ask. After all, the Chamber of Horrors was now no less frightening than the rest of the house.

She stepped forward, opened the door, and shined her flashlight down the stairs. The beam disappeared in blackness.

"Bret?" she called. "You okay?"

Erika, Leslie, and Lynda each cocked an ear toward the open door, but they heard nothing.

Erika tried again: "Bret? You want us to come—"

There was a series of sounds down there in the darkness, sounds of deliberate, purposeful movement, as if Bret were moving something around.

Erika felt a spot of cold grow larger and larger in her chest: fear. She started to call for Bret again, but froze with her mouth open.

There were sounds behind them from somewhere in the house.

The girls turned and listened, their limbs tense, eyes wide, but they couldn't pinpoint the source of the noise.

The sound continued . . . a pounding sound . . . and a voice . . . an angry, muffled voice.

"*Bret!*" Erika barked as she turned back to

the door, trying to sound angry rather than afraid.

There were more sounds deep in the basement—faint, but distinct—but still no response from Bret. The pounding continued behind them.

"Why isn't she answering?" Lynda whispered.

The cold in Erika's chest disappeared quickly. It suddenly occurred to her what was going on down there.

"I was right the first time," she muttered.

"What?" Leslie whispered.

"It's a joke," Erika grumbled through clenched teeth, her voice low with anger, but still with a tremor of fear. "This whole thing is a big, practical joke. And Bret is the one pulling it, just like I thought."

"But how could she?" Leslie whispered. "She doesn't live here anymore, either, you know."

"Yeah, but she doesn't live that far up the coast. It wouldn't have been too hard for her to pull this off, especially if her creepy boyfriend is helping her." Erika leaned into the doorway and shouted, "*Bret!* Either you answer me right now or I'm going to be really ticked off, you hear me?"

Still no reply.

More pounding throughout the house, and that persistent, angry voice, too muffled to understand.

141

"Okay, I'm really ticked at you Bret," Erika snapped, thinking, *and really scared*. She started down the stairs, stomping her feet angrily.

Leslie and Lynda took one more look over their shoulders toward the pounding, glanced at one another, uncertain of what to do, then quickly followed Erika down to the basement, closing the door behind them.

The stairs clunked and clattered beneath their hurried steps until they reached the concrete below, where all three of them came to an abrupt halt.

Leslie began to move her flashlight back and forth slowly as she said, "I really hope she's not going to jump out at us with some—"

Her words were lost in her scream as she threw herself backward away from the face that had suddenly been illuminated by her flashlight.

"It's the Phantom of the Opera, you dweeb," Erika chuckled.

Leslie took a few deep breaths to calm herself.

Erika added, "If you can't take that, we're in trouble, because this room is thick with them, remember?"

"Hey, chill out, okay?" Leslie said. "That scared me to death."

Erika stepped ahead of them and said, "Come on, let's get this over with."

"Get what over with?" Lynda asked.

Erika said, "Kicking Bret's butt into next week."

They walked down the narrow passageway, their flashlight beams crisscrossing one another as they swept back and forth, passing over the sinister faces of the wax monsters that flanked them. Lynda was the only one without a light, and she pressed close to Erika as Leslie walked behind them.

"Bret!" Erika shouted. "Would you just stop whatever you're doing and come *out*! I *mean* it, Bret, I'm *really* upset. This isn't funny anymore. It never *was* funny."

At Erika's prompting, they stopped and listened.

The only sounds they heard were the wind and rain outside; even the sounds of movement deep in the basement had stopped.

Lynda whispered, "Maybe . . . maybe she hurt herself."

"Or maybe she got out," Leslie said.

"She would have let us know if she'd gotten out." Erika started walking again and called, "Bret? Bret!"

They came to the curtained doorway and stopped.

"What do you think is through there?" Lynda whispered.

Erika licked her dry lips and said, "I . . . don't know. It's all so different from the way it was the last time we came down here." Then she shouted, "Okay, Bret, this is your last

143

chance. Unless you never want us to speak to you again, you'd better get out here!''

They waited.

Outside, the wind mourned their predicament mockingly.

Upstairs something continued to pound and grumble in the oppressive darkness of the old house.

''Erika, I don't feel good about this,'' Lynda whispered. ''I think something's wrong. I don't want to go in there.''

''Would you rather go upstairs? To whatever that noise is up there?''

Leslie breathed, ''Let's go on.''

They pushed the curtain aside as they passed through the doorway.

The moment they stepped into the next room, they heard the skittering of more mice over the floor. The sounds shot in every direction and were accompanied by a few tiny squeaks.

''Oh, no. Not again,'' Leslie rasped.

''Bret?'' Erika called. ''Come on, Bret, where *are* you?'' Much of the anger had left her voice, and she tried to speak firmly, but her voice quaked with tension.

The guillotine and gallows towered over them in the shifting light. The shadows gave the appearance of movement to the body hanging from the rope.

''I really . . . *really* don't have a good feeling about this,'' Lynda whispered.

"Bret, I mean it," Erika said, her voice a low, shaky growl. She took a few steps forward, and the other two girls moved with her.

Leslie made a disgusted sound and asked, "What's *this*?"

"What's what?" Erika asked.

"This sticky stuff on the floor."

Then Erika felt it beneath her feet, slick under the soles of her shoes. She turned her flashlight to the floor and saw it, a dark liquid, almost black, spattered here and there around her. She moved the circle of light over the floor, following the substance, until it stopped at the foot of the iron maiden. The maiden was closed. On the floor beside it lay a wax figure of a woman clothed in tattered rags and riddled with bloody holes inflicted on her by the spikes inside the iron maiden. She moved the light backward, realizing that the fluid was almost black . . . but not quite.

It was red.

"Oh, no," she breathed, lifting the flashlight.

She gasped, and the other two girls gave out yelps of surprise. Someone stood a few feet in front of them wearing a black robe with a hood that concealed the face. Both hands were hidden.

The black shape laughed, a high, stifled, girlish titter.

For a moment Erika's tension simply flowed

out of her, and once again she was angry as she moved toward the shape.

"*Damn* you, Bret," she barked, "just *what* do you think you're *doing*, trying to scare us all like that. I am so ticked at you, I may *never* speak to you ag—" She froze when her light illuminated the face that emerged from the hood.

It was not Bret.

It was Mrs. Potter, Karin's mother.

She grinned maniacally as her right hand rose, holding a long knife with dark, glistening streaks on the blade.

For an instant Erika could not move. She was paralyzed where she stood, unable to breathe or speak.

Then she shrieked and pulled herself away from Mrs. Potter, spinning around to face the girls, who were also screaming. She tried to run away, but there was a rush of movement behind her, and a hand closed on her shoulder in an iron grip and jerked her backward.

An arm curled around her throat and squeezed tightly, reducing her scream to a gurgle. Erika clutched her flashlight as if it might save her, and its light was shining on the other two girls, who were backing away from her, screaming, their eyes enormous with fear.

Erika caught a glimpse of the knife's blade slicing downward in front of her and—

It slammed home just below her left shoulder.

In a heartbeat, everything that had been moving so quickly suddenly slowed to a crawl, as if Erika and the others were under water. She felt the knife pulled from her as icy pain exploded in her chest and shoulder. Her knees collapsed, and she felt herself falling against the body behind her, but a hand pushed her away violently, and Erika spun slowly over the concrete, like a ballerina in a dream.

Lynda and Leslie, their screams garbled, throaty sounds, stumbled back through the curtain as Mrs. Potter rushed after them, knife held high, ready to drive into its next victim.

Erika saw the iron maiden as she lurched toward it, saw it coming closer and closer until she slammed against it and slid to the floor.

The iron maiden's door was knocked open.

Something fell heavily on top of Erika.

In spite of her pain, she struggled to get out from under the weight and managed to roll it off her. She dropped her flashlight in the process. It rolled a few inches away from her, and in its light Erika saw Bret. Her mouth and eyes were open in a gory mask of terror. Erika saw the holes . . . the black-red holes all over her face and body.

With a strangled cry of horror, she grabbed the flashlight and pulled it away from Bret. *This can't be happening*, she thought. *That isn't Bret— it's just a wax dummy. This is all some trick, an illusion. It can't be Bret!*

The entire basement exploded with screams,

high, shrill cries of desperation from the girls and roaring demands from Mrs. Potter.

"Come here!" she shouted. "You're not going *anywhere*, not *anymore*! We'll see what good it does you to be pretty and popular *now*!"

Erika tried to sit up, but managed only to prop herself up on her right elbow.

"Run!" she screamed to the girls. "Run and get help! Run and—"

But she interrupted herself with a groan of pain. She knew it wouldn't make any difference if they ran; there was nowhere to go.

The others had gone through the curtain and into the narrow passageway that led to the stairs. Erika could still hear the screams, the struggling.

She put her hand to her wounded shoulder, but it hurt too much. When she pulled it away, it was wearing a deep red glove. Erika felt darkness closing in as she began to lose consciousness.

But the screams in the other part of the basement cut through the pain and haze and forced her to move. She struggled to her feet, pulling herself up the iron maiden; then, hunched forward like a frail old woman, she staggered toward the curtained doorway, making small, animal-like sounds of pain. When she reached the curtain, she clutched it with her free hand, leaned into it too hard, and tore it down around her.

She heard the thunderous sound of several

148

people hurrying down the stairs at the other end of the basement, people with bright lights, men whose voices rumbled into the darkness like soldiers.

Erika tried to hurry forward toward the darting lights, running into wax figures and knocking them to the floor.

A man shouted, "All right, lady, let her go! *Let her go right now!*"

"No!" Mrs. Potter shrieked. "*No*, I *won't* let her go! It's *her* turn, it's *all* their turns now, *all* of them!"

"Let the girl go, lady," another man said, more calmly than the first.

Erika continued down the passageway, panting, swaying as she followed its zigzagging path.

A girl spoke up, her voice frail but shockingly familiar. "No, don't, please don't do it, please, *please* . . ."

Erika hurried. Pain burned through her shoulder and coursed up her neck, down her arms, and deep into the bones of her back. She stumbled around one last corner and fell to the floor.

Three police officers stood at the foot of the stairs, guns drawn.

Mrs. Potter stood with her arm hooked around Lynda's neck and the bloody knife pressed to her throat.

Leslie was sprawled faceup on the floor, propped up on her elbows.

And standing just a few feet in front of Mrs.

Potter was a thin, pale, unhealthy-looking girl whose face shined with tears.

"Please don't hurt her, Momma," Karin said. "Please let her go and put the knife down."

"No, I won't, not until I've done what I set out to do. Because it's not *fair*. Do you hear me, it's *just not fair*!"

In the tension of the moment, no one had noticed Erika on the floor at the opening of the passageway. She turned off her flashlight and slowly, trying not to voice her pain, began to crawl forward, toward Mrs. Potter and Lynda.

"This won't change anything, Momma," Karin said, her voice ragged and thin. "It will just make things worse. You know that, Momma, you *know* that."

Erika got closer . . . slowly closer . . .

"What *I'd* like to know, young lady," Mrs. Potter said angrily, "is what you think you're doing out of your *room*!"

. . . Closer still, Erika locked her eyes on the hem of the black robe and Mrs. Potter's feet beneath it, almost in reach, almost . . .

Karin began to sob, and one of the police officers said, "You'll be facing some serious problems, you hurt that girl, Mrs. Potter."

. . . Inches, just inches to go . . .

"But it's not fair," Mrs. Potter whispered. "It's just not—"

Erika struck. She shot her hand out, clutched

Mrs. Potter's ankle, and pulled as hard as she could.

Mrs. Potter let out a shocked squawk and swung her arms at her sides to keep her balance.

Lynda threw herself forward toward the police officers as Mrs. Potter spun around and fell to her knees, glaring at Erika.

"You! *You!*" Karin's mother screamed, and wrapped both hands around the knife, lifting it over her head, over Erika and—one of the officers shouted, "Don't do it!"

But the knife swung down through the air as Mrs. Potter curled her lips back over her teeth in a hideous grin, and—

A gun fired.

Mrs. Potter slammed forward and hit the ground hard beside Erika, making a small whimpering sound as the knife clattered across the floor.

No one moved for a moment as Erika looked up at them.

Mrs. Potter murmured, "It's not fair . . . it's not fair . . ." over and over again.

Then Leslie got to her feet, crying, "Erika? *Erika!*" She hurried to Erika's side, knelt beside her. "Are you all right? Are you . . . right . . . you all . . . are . . ."

But Leslie's voice faded gradually, and the glare from the policemen's lights dimmed.

Erika lost consciousness.

EPILOGUE

The day of Bret's funeral, Erika lay in her hospital bed, groggy from the painkillers that couldn't quite rid her of the throbbing ache in her chest and shoulder. She ignored the silent television, stared out the window at the stone sky, and thought about Bret.

After passing out in the Chamber of Horrors, Erika had spent a small eternity in blissful oblivion; then she'd awakened in a different kind of chamber of horrors: a recovery room. Her head thick and heavy from anesthesia, Erika was wheeled to her room, where her parents had waited during her surgery. She'd slept for the rest of that day and a good deal of the next.

But she was all too wakeful today.

Bret's mother had been devastated by Bret's death, so much so, in fact, that her ex-husband had had to handle everything. They agreed to have Bret buried there in Dinsmore rather than moving her to Oregon; they both wanted it over with as quickly as possible.

So the funeral was today.

As she stared out the window, her mind returned to the basement of the Waxhouse and, although she fought it, relived what had happened there. She had relived it—gone over it, rethought it, tried to make it turn out right— over and over again since coming out of surgery, and it became more exhausting each time, but she couldn't fight it off. What haunted her most was the anger she'd felt toward Bret for pulling what Erika had been certain was another practical joke. Guilt clenched her throat when she remembered the way she'd shouted and sworn at Bret as she walked deeper into the basement, while Bret's dead body was hidden away in the iron maiden.

The pain she felt when she thought of that was far worse than the pain in her shoulder, and she knew it would take much longer to heal.

She'd been so busy going over those few minutes that had seemed so long, she'd taken little time to ask herself or her parents exactly what had *happened* down there in the Chamber of Horrors. Why had Mrs. Potter *done* such a thing? What reason could she possibly have had to kill Bret and to try to kill Erika?

All Erika knew was that Mrs. Potter was in the same hospital as she, recovering from the gunshot wound that had narrowly prevented Erika's death.

But she still did not know *why* . . .

Erika awoke later—although she didn't know how much later—to the sound of a soft voice. She opened her eyes, blinked away the blur, and saw a pale, gaunt Karin smiling down at her. The smile was a painful one, but warm. She was a different Karin altogether. Although much thinner than she had been six years ago, she did not look healthy; in fact, she appeared sickly, as if she hadn't been out in the sun in ages, got no exercise and ate next to nothing. Her face was pockmarked and drawn, and her hair was still stringy. She took Erika's hand and squeezed it.

Leslie and Lynda stood behind her and smiled sadly at Erika over her shoulder. All of them had red, puffy eyes and cheeks glossy with half-dried tears. They smelled of cold winter air and faint perfume. When Erika finally spoke, her voice sounded for a moment like cellophane crackling dryly.

"Karin," she said, "we all thought you—"

"I know," Karin interrupted, patting Erika's hand. "And I'm sorry about that. I'm really sorry." She still had that odd way of talking:

bowing her head nervously, speaking in a hushed, nervous tone, blinking rapidly now and then. "That's . . . that's why I'm here."

"It's good to see you," Erika whispered.

"How are you feeling?" Leslie asked.

"I'm not feeling much, really," Erika slurred with a half-smile. "I'm full of drugs."

"Well," Lynda said, "not feeling much is better than . . . not feeling at all, right?" She seemed to regret her words as soon as she spoke them and sucked her lips between her teeth as she lowered her eyes.

"You went to the funeral?" Erika asked.

They all nodded, but said nothing.

"Where are my parents?" Erika asked.

"They're in the cafeteria right now," Leslie replied. "They'll be back in a little while. They wanted us to tell you that Rick's on his way here now. He'll arrive later this afternoon."

Erika felt herself relax a little at that news; she looked forward to seeing him. She noticed a shoe box tucked under Karin's left arm. It looked old and a bit tattered on the corners.

"What's that?" Erika asked.

"Something I wanted to show you guys," she said.

Leslie said, "She wouldn't tell us what it was until we got here. She said it was for all of us."

Karin nodded. "I know that . . . well, you have a lot of questions, all of you. About . . . about my mother. You've been too polite to ask them, and . . . well, so much has hap-

155

pened . . . it's been chaos, and I suppose maybe you haven't *thought* to ask them, but . . . some of the answers are in this box."

The girls suddenly became very serious. "You don't have to," Lynda said.

"Yeah, really," Leslie added, "it's okay if you just want to drop it."

Erika managed a heavy, sedated chuckle. "The whole time, we were thinking it was those weird guys over at the store."

"The Cromleys?" Karin smiled. "No. Mr. Cromley's crazy, spends most of his time sitting in his chair laughing at nothing, but he's harmless. His boys, though, you have to keep an eye on their hands, if you know what I mean. But this . . . I want to, really. I won't feel right if I don't."

As Karin pulled a chair over to the side of the bed, the other girls exchanged tense and curious glances.

"Everything I'm about to tell you," Karin went on, "I've already told the police and the doctors caring for my mother. When she's well enough, she'll be taken to another hospital. Another . . . *kind* of hospital. There will be a trial and everything. I'll have to repeat all of this over and over again. But telling you guys . . . this is more important than all that. In fact, telling you will feel like . . . well, like telling it all for the very first time."

She placed the box on the bedside stand and

removed the lid. After rummaging through its contents for a moment, she removed a photograph and handed it to Erika.

Leslie and Lynda went to the opposite side of the bed and looked at the photograph with Erika.

It was a black-and-white picture of a stunningly beautiful young woman leaning against an enormous redwood. She wore a checkered shirt and a pair of denim shorts, and her dark hair fell around her shoulders in beautiful waves and curls. Her smile was broad and her teeth straight; her eyes, even in black and white, were bright. She looked vital and eager and, most of all, naturally and perfectly beautiful.

Karin handed over another photograph, this one of the same woman but in color. She wore a lovely wedding gown and stood beside her bridesmaid, smiling but noticeably nervous.

Another photograph, again in color: the same woman, lying in a bed, looking more mature but just as beautiful, perhaps even more so, and cradling a tiny red-faced baby in her arms.

Then Karin handed Erika a jarring picture of a car accident, this one in *too much* color. Two cars were heaped in the middle of the road, both so mangled, it was difficult to tell where one car stopped and the other began. There were two garish puddles of blood on the pavement among all the debris.

Then there was a picture of someone lying in a hospital bed, face covered with bandages.

Then a picture of Karin's mother.

"She was beautiful once," Karin said, her voice nearly a whisper. "The car accident happened when I was just a baby. She doesn't even look the same to me in these pictures. I only knew her with the scar . . . and the new face. They had to do some constructive surgery, so I guess you could call it a new face. But not as pretty as the old one, that's for sure. And she always knew that. It ate at her. Daddy used to tell me—when she wasn't around to hear, of course—that before the accident she was a much nicer person, much warmer, always happy. He told me those things to assure me it wasn't my fault that she . . . behaved the way she did."

Karin took a deep breath and let it out slowly as she looked at the picture of her mother as a young woman, leaning against a tree and grinning.

"She would get mad easily," she continued. "Sometimes for no reason at all. And sometimes . . . sometimes she would hit me. Beat me. Daddy would try to stop her, but it only made her worse. She would turn on *him*, start yelling at him, screaming that he didn't love her anymore, that he *hated* her . . . that he hated her because she wasn't pretty anymore . . . because she was ugly. And about then she'd point to me and scream, 'Ugly like *her*!'"

She took the pictures and put them back in the box, muttering, "I was ugly even then. I was *always* ugly."

Erika closed her eyes and tried not to let herself imagine too vividly what Karin's life must have been like.

"Daddy was my only friend then," she said, "my ally. Until he died. Or . . . was killed. Murdered."

Lynda gasped.

"Momma had gotten worse by then. She'd gotten to the point where she'd stalk around the house sometimes, mumbling to herself about what a beauty she'd once been, but not anymore, and now she'd passed it on to her little girl, and her husband hated her for it, didn't love her anymore, probably went around ogling beautiful women on the street. She was that way on the day Daddy worked on the wiring in the hall. He'd turned off the main switch, of course, so he wouldn't get electrocuted. But . . . well, you can probably figure it out yourselves. Momma turned it back on. While I was standing there watching him work."

"Why didn't you tell someone?" Erika asked.

"Too scared. Momma told me not to worry, that we'd get along fine, just the two of us. We didn't need anybody's help, and nobody wanted to help ugly people, anyway. That was almost all she talked about . . . how we were ugly . . . how there were probably lots of other ugly people in town, the country, the world . . . how nobody liked ugly people . . . nobody anywhere . . .''

Erika felt an ache in the pit of her stomach. She had felt guilty before because of what she'd said to Karin, but there was no word for how she felt now. Karin had heard nothing from her mother except how ugly she was. Then she'd come to Erika hoping, maybe even expecting, to hear something else, but . . .

''Anyway,'' Karin went on, ''she slowly got worse. Just a little at a time, but it was noticeable. She started staying in more. She tried to keep me in, but I had to go to school, of course. And then I met you guys.'' A smile broke through the tension in the room. She looked so thin and unhealthy that smiling seemed a painful act for her. ''But . . . well, I never told you, of course, but . . . Momma didn't like you. She had no reason, no *real* reason, anyway. But she thought she did. She said you were just laughing at me behind my back, that you weren't really my friends, that you just wanted me around so . . . you could laugh at me. I didn't believe her. *Wouldn't* believe her. I knew you weren't like that. You were always so nice to me, all of you. In fact, you made me happier than I'd been since my daddy died. But . . . she didn't like it.

''She started making me come straight home from school. She told me I couldn't spend any time with you. I tried to sneak some in, but I always ended up running home because . . . I got scared. I was scared she'd catch me and . . . beat me. Or, worse yet, lock me in the hall closet. She did that a lot. She used to tell me to sit in the dark and think about how grateful I was to have someone like her for a mother, someone who understood what it was like to be ugly.

"Then she took me out of school and . . . well, I guess it seemed I just dropped off the face of the earth, huh? She taught me herself with some correspondence course. It was awful. And . . . I missed you guys so much.

"Word got around that you were all leaving. I found out you were meeting at the Waxhouse and decided to go even though I might get into trouble for it. And when I went . . . well, you remember the little fit I had. I never apologized for that, and I'm sorry. But . . . I hope you understand now."

"Of course we do," Erika slurred, taking Karin's hand.

"Well, Momma caught me coming back from my visit with you and grilled me for information. I told her, and she punished me, as usual. But what wasn't usual was that I talked back that time. I told her you were my friends and I missed you, and that in six years from that day we were all going to get together again at the Waxhouse. Oh, boy, did she laugh. She laughed for a long time. Then she said,

161

'They're not your friends, and you're not getting together with them ever.' She never said any more about it.

"A couple of years after you left, Mrs. Wattenberg died, and—talk about shocking—Momma went over to the Waxhouse to lend support and give a hand to Mr. Wattenberg. She went over there a lot, in fact.

"Then, a couple years after that—no, maybe closer to three—Mr. Wattenberg, who'd been failing fast ever since his wife died, had to go into the hospital. Momma was one of his best friends by then. She offered to take care of the house for him until he came back. But he never came back. He's in a rest home right now, just getting worse and worse."

"What were you doing during that time?" Leslie asked.

"Same as usual. I could probably count on one hand the number of times I left the house. And I was still making regular trips to that hall closet when I did or said something that smacked of disloyalty or mutiny. See, she saw us as two poor ugly people against the mean world, and she said we had to stick together. But I was getting pretty sneaky, and a little bit at a time I was planning my exit."

Lynda said, "So, your mother nailed up those boards over the windows at the Waxhouse?"

"And put all those locks on the doors?" Leslie asked.

Karin nodded. "See, I knew the day was coming, and it was really bugging me that I probably wouldn't be able to make it, so I was very upset. But then it occurred to me . . . maybe *that* was why Momma had been so friendly with Mr. Wattenberg. Maybe she had something planned, all that time, that far ahead. So I made plans, too. I figured if she was going to do anything, she'd lock me in the closet. She usually did that when she left the house, anyway. So I hid a flashlight in there. And a screwdriver. I didn't mention anything about the reunion, wondering if maybe *she'd* bring it up. She didn't. But sure enough, come that day, she locked me up. I was ready. At least, I *thought* I was.

"Once she had me in the closet, she stayed outside the door. I could hear her doing something. I could hear something clattering against the door, but I didn't know what it was. Yet. When I heard her leave, I turned on my flashlight, got my screwdriver, and went to work on the doorknob. I got it off, popped the spring with the screwdriver, and . . . the door wouldn't open. She'd put another lock on the outside. A hasp and a padlock. So I started throwing myself against that door. I don't know, I just had a bad feeling, a feeling something awful was going to happen, or maybe had already happened. I threw myself against the door for what seemed like forever. I guess I might have run out of air for a while, because I think I lost consciousness. But I'm not sure. Anyway, I finally broke that hasp and got out of the closet. I called the police, they came and got me, and we went to the Waxhouse. But . . .''

Karin leaned forward and put her elbows on her thighs. Her head drooped heavily.

''. . . I was too late,'' she breathed through tears that had come suddenly. ''I'm sorry. I'm so . . . *so* sorry.''

Lynda and Leslie went to her, comforted her.

''It wasn't your fault,'' Erika said.

''Of *course* it wasn't,'' Lynda added.

''What's important is that you're okay,'' Leslie said, putting an arm around her.

''I don't know if I'll ever be all right again,'' Karin replied. ''Not after what Momma's done.''

''She's sick, Karin,'' Erika said. ''Sounds like she's been sick for a long time. And there's nothing you could have done about that.''

Karin sniffled and lifted her head. ''Maybe she's sick. But maybe she's not so sick after all. For most of my life I've felt the same way she does: that to get anybody to like me, to deserve anybody's respect or affection, I have to look a certain way, I have to be pretty. She used to be pretty, but when she lost her looks, she kept thinking that way, and it drove her crazy. If she was sick, that *made* her sick. But I never *was* pretty. If I were to go on thinking the way she did . . . what would *I* have become?''

164

Rain began to spatter the window quietly, and the girls said nothing for a while. Finally Erika spoke.

"You're going to be fine, Karin," she said. "You're going to be just fine. And if you keep telling yourself *that*, if you keep thinking *that* way, I know *exactly* what you'll become. Just fine."

ABOUT THE AUTHOR

As a high school English teacher, Joseph Locke often wrote stories for his classes. Encouraged by his students and his wife, he stopped teaching and started writing with publication in mind while he worked as a part-time salesman. Less than one year later, he began to write full-time. He and his wife live in Eureka, California, where he is working on his next novel.

Farley Mowat

Chronicler of man against the elements.

Bestselling author, Farley Mowat, portrays true-life adventure and survival with unique passion. His courageous stories of remote lands, people and animals have been read in over twenty languages in more than forty countries.

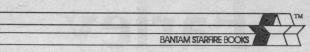

Intriguing Fiction for Teens

☐ **IN LANE THREE, ALEX ARCHER** by Tessa Duder
29020-7 $3.50/$3.99C
Fifteen-year-old Alex Archer has spent six years training to represent New Zealand as a freestyle swimmer at the 1960 Olympic Games—but so has her arch rival, Maggie Benton. Alex's quest becomes more difficult as she learns what it means to love and to lose—in racing and in her life. She learns, the hard way, what it takes to become a champion.

☐ **SAVING LENNY** by Margaret Willey
29204-8 $3.50/$3.99C
Lenny and Jesse are madly in love, and Jesse has never felt so adored or so needed. She soon learns that Lenny has serious problems stemming from a history of chronic depression. Jesse is convinced she can help, but their relationship deteriorates as Lenny's depression deepens. In trying to save Lenny, Jesse is in danger of losing herself.

☐ **NECESSARY PARTIES** by Barbara Dana
26984-4 $3.50/$3.99C
Fifteen-year-old Chris Mills loves his parents, but he hates the fact that they want a divorce. Chris knows that they just haven't tried hard enough to make their marriage work. Determined to fight the divorce, Chris does the only thing he can to keep his family together: he sues his parents!